SEDUCING AN HEIRESS ON A TRAIN

A *Victorian Christmas Story*

LAUREN SMITH

This book is a work of fiction. Names, characters, places, and incidents are the product of the author's imagination or are used fictitiously. Any resemblance to actual events, locales, or persons, living or dead, is coincidental.

Copyright © 2019 by Lauren Smith

Tempted by a Rogue excerpt Copyright © 2015 by Lauren Smith

The League of Rogues (R) is a federally registered trademark owned by Lauren Smith and cannot be copied or used without the expression permission of Lauren Smith.

All rights reserved. In accordance with the U.S. Copyright Act of 1976, the scanning, uploading, and electronic sharing of any part of this book without the permission of the publisher constitutes unlawful piracy and theft of the author's intellectual property. If you would like to use material from the book (other than for review purposes), prior written permission must be obtained by contacting the publisher at lauren@laurensmithbooks.com. Thank you for your support of the author's rights.

The publisher is not responsible for websites (or their content) that are not owned by the publisher.

*L*ondon, *December 1888*

The ticking clock in the corner of the waiting area counted down the seconds toward Oliver Conway's doom. Each second sounded like a hammer fall in the interminable silence. He clenched his worn black gloves in one hand and held his hat in the other as he waited to be summoned. Finally, the door to the bank president's office opened, and a portly man with kind eyes glanced down the hall to find him.

"Lord Conway, I will see you now."

Oliver swallowed and stood, then straightened his shoulders and entered the office of Mr. Kelly, president of Drummonds Bank.

"Please, sit, Lord Conway." Mr. Kelly waved at the pair of leather chairs facing the desk.

Oliver sat, his hands trembling a little. At the grown

age of one and thirty he had few reasons to be afraid, but today this man held the fate of Oliver's family's future in his hands.

Mr. Kelly removed a pair of spectacles from his coat pocket and nestled them on the bridge of his nose. He pulled a stack of papers toward him. "I've reviewed all of the accounts this morning, my lord, and I'm afraid the loans your father extended two years ago are past due. I received the payments you've been sending, but it barely covers the interest currently owed."

Oliver's heart sank, and a bitter taste filled his mouth. "And the stock he purchased? We authorized the bank with permission to sell. What amount did it bring in?"

Mr. Kelly sighed, and his gray eyes, still showing that damnable sincerity and kindness, only increased Oliver's fears.

"The stock was worthless after the businesses your father invested in went bankrupt. I was able to recuperate a small amount, but it covered only the interest owed for the next month's payment."

Panic spread through Oliver. He had been fighting for over a year to save his family and his home from ruin after his father's death, and now all he had was his name and the title of Viscount Conway, which at the moment was a burden almost beyond what he could bear.

"Mr. Kelly, is there no way...?"

The banker removed his spectacles and set them on the desk. He leaned forward, his voice lowering.

"I have so few options, Oliver. Your father was a dear friend and..." Mr. Kelly paused, collecting himself. "But my hands are tied by bank regulations and investor expectations."

"So that's it, then? Astley Court, all of the tenancy properties and everything we own..."

"Will be property of Drummonds in thirty days," Mr. Kelly finished. "You've done a commendable job, but the debts were simply too great. The only way to..." Mr. Kelly stopped and shook his head.

"What?" Oliver pressed. "What were you about to say? I will do anything."

"The only option I see as a way out of this mess is to, shall we say...marry advantageously?"

Oliver didn't quite comprehend the banker's words because they were so unexpected. "Pardon?"

"An heiress, dear boy," Mr. Kelly said, forgetting their difference in social standing for a moment, not that Oliver cared.

"An heiress," he muttered, finding the implication distasteful.

"Yes. Find a pretty young lady with a fortune to her name and secure her hand in less than thirty days, and you will have access to money. I could get around some of the resistance here if you returned before the middle of January with a rich bride upon your arm."

Oliver stared down at his worn-out gloves and top

hat, which rested in his lap. So it had come to this. Sell himself to the highest-bidding lady in London and find himself saddled with a wife, one he might not like, let alone love—all to save his home and family.

"Do it for Astley Court. Do it for your mother."

The thought of his mother, his younger brother Everett, and his sister Zadie all depending on him. It was all it took to make him decide.

"Thirty days," Oliver said, as if sealing the pact.

Still feeling like a man doomed and facing the gallows, Oliver thanked Mr. Kelly and shook his hand before he exited the office. He pulled on his gloves and cursed as he found yet another small hole in the leather. He had spent the last year putting every bit of coin he had toward the business debts his father's investments had accrued. The cost of his efforts, aside from his pride, had been clothing three years too old, and showing every day of it.

His mother and sister had suffered more, being forced to wear gowns well out of fashion. He and Everett were able to get by on what they owned since men's fashions changed far less and more slowly than the fashions of ladies. Zadie had held her head high, even when other girls had mocked her during her debut this season when she'd worn an outmoded gown.

His family had also reduced the staff at their country estate by half and had sold their large townhouse in London six months ago. Now they only rented rooms when in town for the season. Oliver didn't want to think about what cuts they would have to make if he wasn't able to save Astley Court. A man without land and without a fortune... He shuddered, but resolved himself to the idea of learning a trade. He was not opposed to it, but the social circles his family ran in would surely find it distasteful, which meant he put Everett's and Zadie's futures at risk.

But if he could find an heiress...

No. He *would* find an heiress. He would do his duty, in whatever form that required.

As he left Drummonds and stepped out into the streets, someone called his name.

"Conway!"

He spun to find a man striding toward him, waving his arm. The tall, dark-haired fellow had the same green eyes as him.

"Cousin!" He laughed as he shook Devon St. Laurent's hand. Devon was second in line to become the Duke of Essex. Oliver's great-grandfather, Godric St. Laurent, and his wife Emily had had four children, and Devon's grandfather, second eldest of the brood, was the current duke.

"Care for a drink? I was heading to Berkley's."

"I would love to, but I surrendered my membership three months ago." It was one of the many frivolous luxuries both he and Everett had removed to slim down their family's expenses.

"What? Why?"

Oliver sighed. "It is a long story." His shoulders

ached now. He had been waiting to see Mr. Kelly for over an hour, and he had been strung tighter than an archer's bow the entire time.

Devon smiled and clapped a hand on Oliver's shoulder. "Come on, we'll drink at a pub nearby, and you can tell me this long story."

Half an hour later, the two of them were two pints into a nice afternoon.

"All right, Oliver, tell me what's the matter." Devon's expression was back to that of concern. And like they had been as boys, Oliver found his trust in his cousin well placed as he shared his family's dire financial straits.

"Lord, Oliver, that's dreadful. Why don't you speak to my grandfather? I'm sure he wouldn't mind helping you out. You know how he loves Astley Court."

"I know," Oliver admitted. His great-uncle, the Duke of Essex, was a loving man, openhearted and kind, but even he did not possess the funds to help the Conways out of their massive debt.

"Why not?" Devon pressed. He rolled his half-empty pint glass between his hands.

"It wouldn't be enough. The amount we need to pay... It would put Essex House at risk. I cannot ask that."

Devon's eyes darkened. "It's truly that bad?"

"It is," Oliver replied numbly. He glanced around the pub, noting the men who sought to escape the winter chill. Most were laughing and talking, all in seemingly good spirits. It only served to deepen his melancholy.

"I feel I've failed," Oliver whispered.

"You haven't." Devon leaned forward and set his glass down on the table. "Debts happen, businesses fail. Your father made these choices, and they seemed good and sound at the time. It isn't your fault they failed. The world changed, and we're all still trying to catch up with it."

Oliver drained the rest of his pint, letting the stout ale go to his head. His stomach was empty, and his head ached from the lack of food. He had done his best not to eat at too many restaurants while he was in London. The expense was one more thing he couldn't afford.

"The banker said I need to find an heiress. Can you believe that? It was his *professional* advice."

"An heiress?" Delight suddenly burst on Devon's face as he grinned. "That may be something I could help you with."

"Oh?"

"You remember Adelaide Berwick?"

"The Earl of Berwick's daughter?" He nodded. He had spent much of his youth around the girl. She chattered endlessly and could be quite mean-spirited sometimes.

"She still wants you, Oliver. I know you didn't offer for her when she came out last year, but she is still hoping you'll change your mind. Her father has settled a hefty sum on her as a dowry and a large sum to be given as an inheritance if he approves of the match. Old Berwick always liked you."

The Earl of Berwick was a good fellow, but his wife and his only daughter could both be unbearable. Still, Oliver considered it.

"Adelaide is a bit...much, don't you think?" he asked his cousin.

Devon shrugged. "Yes, I suppose she is. But she's as rich as Croesus, and that's what you need, isn't it?" His cousin chuckled. "Besides, if she truly drove you mad, you could always live apart in separate homes. That seems to be quite acceptable these days with those who marry out of necessity."

"I suppose you're right. I could stomach it. For Astley Court."

"There you are then. Cheer up. You're coming to Lady Poole's ball tonight, aren't you? Adelaide will be there. Propose to her, and I'll go with you to procure a special license. You'll be married by Christmas."

"Married to Adelaide Berwick by Christmas..." Oliver shook his head, trying not to laugh at the maddening twist his life had taken.

"Married, at least," Devon replied. "That ought to be some consolation."

They finished their drinks, and Devon paid the barman. They then donned their gloves and hats before embracing the chill outside.

"Shall I see you tonight?"

"You shall." Oliver shook Devon's hand and parted

ways with his cousin. He walked to the hotel his family were renting rooms at while they were in town. The Grosvenor Hotel on Buckingham Palace Road was an impressive structure modeled in the Baroque interpretation of French Renaissance architectural style. His father had been a good friend of the hotel's current owner, and whenever they stayed in town, they were able to rent a room far cheaper than most guests, for which Oliver was extremely grateful. It didn't hurt that having a titled lord staying there caused a flurry of interest from other guests, which the owner thought was good for business.

As Oliver entered its opulent entryway, his eyes rolled over the fluted twisting columns and the way the light from the chandeliers turned the white marble a soft gold. Bright-red roses filled half a dozen large crystal vases, and a group of young ladies in colorful gowns were gossiping as they donned their velvet manteaux, likely for an evening out at the opera or perhaps a ball. More than one lady in the group caught Oliver's eye, offering him a blushing smile before they dissolved into giggles with their friends as he passed.

In another life, Oliver would've enjoyed the attention. He was no fool. He had his mother's fair looks as well as his father's, and more than one young lady had thrown herself at him over the years. He had thoroughly enjoyed seducing a few, though never too far, just enough to please his ego and give the lady a breathtaking memory.

But he was older now, and there was a part of him that did long to settle down. He wanted what his mother and father had, a marriage based on love and respect.

But I won't have that with Adelaide. She will own me, and she'll never let me forget it.

He climbed the stairs to the third floor and then headed down the hall to the suite of rooms he'd rented. As he opened the door, he saw his mother and sister in the sitting room, talking excitedly about tonight.

"Oh, Oliver!" his mother exclaimed in joy as she saw him. She rose and came over to embrace him. "How was Mr. Kelly? Did he give us a very long extension?"

Oliver's gut knotted as he carefully planned his response. He saw his little sister, Zadie, who was only eighteen, watching him with anxious eyes.

She knows. She's always been able to read me like an open book.

"Mother, perhaps you should sit down."

His mother, still lovely even at fifty-two, now became concerned. "Oliver... What's the matter? What did Mr. Kelly say?"

Zadie gently ushered their mother into a chair, and then she stood behind it, as strong as a soldier in Her Majesty's army.

"Where is Everett?" he asked.

"Here." His brother stepped out of the nearest bedroom. Everett could be Oliver's twin, though he was three years younger. He'd removed his coat and was waiting for Oliver to speak. They all were.

"Mr. Kelly could not grant us an extension. The entire amount of the debt has been called in, and we are destitute. We have thirty days to set our affairs in order and arrange for the sale of Astley Court and all of its sub properties, as well as the furnishings in the house."

That bitter taste had returned, and it broke his heart to see his mother wipe the tears in her eyes. No matter what Devon had said, he knew he had failed his family.

"I haven't given up," Oliver told them. "I have one last chance. Mr. Kelly suggested it, and I shall endeavor to do my best."

"What is it?" his mother asked. Even though her husband had passed more than a year ago, she, like Her Majesty, still mourned her husband and had not shed her widow's weeds. Her black silk gown whispered against the carpets as she stood and faced him with a strength that made him proud.

"If I can marry an heiress before the middle of next January, we'll be able to save the house, tenancies...all of it."

"An heiress? Oh, Oliver, no." His mother shook her head. "I'll not have you become some dreadful fortune hunter."

"I won't be, Mother. I already know the woman I'm choosing, and she won't require any hunting." He tried to smile, but he knew the expression failed to reach his eyes. "You could even say that she's been hunting me."

"Who would be...?" Zadie asked, and then her eyes widened with horror. "Oh no, Oliver, not her. *Anyone* but her."

"Zadie." He held up a hand, trying to reassure her. "She's not that terrible."

"Not that terrible? She covered my hair in tar when I was twelve, Oliver. Mother had to cut it all off. I looked like a boy for almost a year!"

"Bloody hell," Everett said, then whistled. "I forgot Adelaide did that."

"She was just a girl then," Oliver said.

Everett shook his head in disgust. "Choose anyone but that one. There must be other heiresses."

"Everett, heiresses do not grow on trees," their mother said coldly. "If Oliver believes Adelaide is our only choice, then we must bear it." When Everett made a gagging noise, she added, "Or *you* could marry her." At which point, Everett turned as white as alabaster.

Zadie sank into the chair their mother had now vacated, while Everett shot Oliver a sympathetic look as their mother took his hands in hers and gave a gentle squeeze.

"You truly want this?" Margaret asked him.

Oliver squeezed her hands back. "Mother, it's not what I want, but it is what must be done. I won't lose our home, and I won't put Zadie's and Everett's futures at risk. They need a stable life and a reputation unsullied by destitution if they are to make decent matches."

For a long moment, no one said anything. Then his mother cupped his cheek and tried to smile. "You are a wonderful son to make such a sacrifice. I would give anything to keep you from doing this."

"I know, Mother." He closed his eyes, drew a deep breath, and tried to summon a smile. "Now, we have Lady Poole's ball tonight, and I for one would like to enjoy myself this evening before I propose."

He would not let himself think about what his future might be. Certainly not tonight with his last night of freedom before he shackled himself to an unwanted heiress.

❧ 2 ❧

Rayne Egerton tried to quell the rise of nerves that fluttered in her belly as her father helped her down from their coach. Her father, Douglas Egerton, beamed at her with pride. She tried to smile back.

"Breathe, my dear. You'll do just fine. None of these ladies are any more special than you."

Rayne wished her father's words could comfort her, but the truth was, she felt out of place in England. They had only just arrived from a steamer ship out of New York, and London was proving to be more intimidating than New York had ever been. As much as she liked the country, the people seemed far less welcoming than she'd hoped. Even Americans with all their money weren't always welcome...or perhaps it was because of it?

"It's my first English ball, Father. What if I don't

know the right dances or say the wrong thing to one of the peers? The titles still confuse me." She had spent the last month reading a copy of *Debrett's Peerage* as she tried to understand the complicated system. Rayne still felt completely uncomfortable with all of the modes of address. At home, a woman was either a *Miss* or a *Mrs.*, and a man was simply a *Mr.* There were no earls, dukes, viscount, barons, or knights. Here it was all *Lord this* or *Right Honorable that*. And trying to keep their order of importance straight... It was all too much.

A footman at the door ushered them into Lady Poole's extravagant home. Great chandeliers lit the entry hall as she and her father joined the other newly arrived guests. She removed her ivory-colored silk-and-velvet dolman, something that resembled a half-coat and half-cape with its loose, sling-like sleeves. She unhooked the fastener at her neck and allowed the footman to slip it off and put it away for her. Her father had insisted on the new costly wardrobe before they had left for England. He'd had the gowns ordered from the House of Worth in Paris. It had embarrassed her to have such expensive things, but her father said they would be judged quite harshly based on their clothing. He'd reminded her that they would have to work twice as hard to fit in with the social crowd of London during the season.

To make the best impression, she had chosen a pale-rose evening gown with a low square neckline and sleeves that clung to the edges of her shoulders. Her gown was trimmed with live roses that had been carefully sewn in over the embroidered silk rosebuds on her skirts, draping from the high bustle at the back down to the front of her gown. A red silk bow exited the middle of her bustle, catching the viewer's eye to the pale-pink gown. It was exquisite, but Rayne wasn't used to such things, and she certainly didn't feel like she belonged in it.

At home in New York, she'd worn more serviceable, sensible clothes because she spent a great deal of time assisting her father at his office. She was fortunate to have a father who believed women were capable of working alongside men, but he was the exception. Most men in New York had laughed at her attempts to discuss business and politics, and she was afraid London would be no different.

As she and her father entered the ballroom, dozens of women were already eyeing her, whispering behind raised fans, their eyes glittering with curiosity or malice. She knew why—she was an American heiress, and every unattached man in the room would soon find a way to manage an introduction to her. It was a common practice now for the titled men of England to seek marriages with rich American heiresses. And that was the very last thing Rayne wanted, for a man to see her simply as a bank account. She didn't care if the man was a duke—if he was a fortune hunter, she wanted nothing to do with him.

She kept her arm tucked in her father's, and her

other hand clutched her skirts as they moved through the thick crowds. There had to be close to seventy people inside the room. Musicians played in a distant corner, and waiters moved around the edges of the crowd, offering champagne to those not partaking in the dance. Rayne watched the dancers, trying to recognize the steps, wondering how best to match them. The only dance she felt comfortable with was the waltz.

"Mr. Egerton!" Lady Poole came over, beaming at them both. She had met Rayne's father a few months ago while in New York and had sent them invitations the moment she discovered they would be visiting England.

Her father bowed, and Rayne dipped into a curtsy. "Lady Poole." The fashionable Englishwoman was in her midforties and still quite stunning. The soft smile she cast toward Douglas didn't go unnoticed by Rayne. She'd wondered over the last year if her father and Lady Poole's frequent letters to one another might be leading to something more. If he found happiness again after losing his wife, Rayne was ready to support his decision to remarry. All the more so if he chose Lady Poole.

"How are you faring, Rayne, dear?" Lady Poole asked. Rayne smiled in genuine relief at having at least one ally here.

"A bit nervous, I admit."

"That's quite normal." Lady Poole tapped her closed fan in her palm. "Let's see if I can't make some introductions." She took Rayne from her father's arm and then towed her quickly around the room, introducing her to all the ladies in attendance. The names and titles became a confusing blur by the end.

"Stay here while I fetch some gentlemen to fill your dance card, my dear." She left Rayne at a spot near the wall with a group of other young ladies. They all shared sympathetic looks with her.

Rayne tried not to lose herself in shame as she watched a number of handsome young bucks prowl by her and the others left out of the dancing.

Heavens...I've become a wallflower so soon.

"Oh dear." The girl next to her shuffled her feet anxiously. "She's coming. Buck up, ladies," the girl hissed in warning to her fellow flowers.

"Who?" Rayne asked the girl, her stomach knotting with dread.

"Adelaide Berwick. Whatever you do, don't show any hint of weakness," the girl replied and raised her chin defiantly as a pretty young woman around Rayne's age came up to the group of single ladies. A trio of girls followed on Adelaide's heels, all twittering behind their fans.

"Well, 'tis a pity Lady Poole did not invite more young men. Quite silly to have so many left desiring partners. There's simply *nothing* worse than being a wall-flower," she declared. Her soft blue silk gown, Rayne noted, looked as expensive as hers, but it lacked the flair of the roses. Adelaide seemed to notice this and sneered at Rayne.

"I do believe you're wilting." She pointed her fan at Rayne's dress. Rayne almost looked down but didn't. Even if the freshly cut roses were wilting, she didn't want to give the girl the satisfaction. She knew how she would respond in America, but here? She was well out of her depth.

Adelaide changed the subject. "I'm afraid we're not acquainted. You aren't familiar to me. Let me guess... A country cousin of Lady Poole's? She is always so charitable." Adelaide's friends giggled.

Rayne bit the side of her cheek. *Do not respond. You will embarrass Father.*

"Oh dear. Have you lost your tongue?" Adelaide continued. "The country mouse is too timid."

Rayne curled her fingers around her own fan, inwardly imagining bringing it down upon Adelaide's head.

"I have a tongue, Miss Berwick. You're simply not worth the breath or the words to speak to."

The wallflowers behind Rayne all gasped. Adelaide's brown eyes narrowed to angry slits. She tossed her auburn curls venomously.

"You are American, of course. You must be the daughter of that rich old man everyone is fussing over tonight. Well, lesson one, *American*. I'm the daughter of Lord Berwick, so you will address me as Lady Adelaide, not *miss*." Her smugness was short-lived because Rayne was good and furious now at the girl's dig at her father. No one insulted him, especially not some twit like this.

Rayne took a step closer, plastering a smile upon her face. "My apologies, Lady Adelaide. I didn't see an earl's daughter here, only a spoiled little brat."

Adelaide bared her teeth as she readied a response, but Rayne wasn't done. She raised her voice a little so the girls behind her all heard.

"Be careful what you say next, Lady Adelaide, or I might ask my father to purchase everything you own. As you said, I'm the daughter of a very rich American. My father could buy half this country on a lark if it suited him."

Adelaide's face went ghostly white, and then her pretty face pinched and her cheeks turned a bright red.

"All the money in the world doesn't fix poor breeding," she snapped.

"I suppose you would know, seeing as how most old families in England are inbred," Rayne shot back without a second thought.

Adelaide looked ready to spew fire, but the trio of girls behind her pulled her away, steering her toward the table of refreshments. Rayne released a sigh of relief.

"You Americans really are as bold as brass, as they say," the girl next to her said. She had stunning green eyes and dark-brown hair.

"I realize that may have been very foolish." Rayne blushed. Her temper was cooling, and as it did, rationality and doubt returned, along with embarrassment. She had just threatened the daughter of an earl. That wouldn't go over well.

LAUREN SMITH

"Could you truly do it?" the girl asked.

"Do what?" Rayne replied.

"Buy her family's estate and property like that?"

"Perhaps. What does her father earn in any given year?" She blushed again at the inappropriate question. The English thought it was so crass to talk openly of money.

"About forty thousand a year."

Rayne didn't even hesitate. "Oh yes, definitely. Twice over, I should think."

The wallflowers gathered around her then, all gasping and chattering questions all at once.

"Ladies, let her breathe," the green-eyed girl exclaimed. "My name is Zadie, by the way. It's a pleasure to meet you."

"The same," Rayne replied, relaxing a little at Zadie's warm smile. "I'm Rayne Egerton."

"Rayne, you told off Lady Adelaide, and that makes you my new favorite friend."

"I take it she terrorizes you all often?"

"Often," Zadie agreed with a frown. "She's the worst sort of aristocrat. Not all ladies in her station are like that. I hope you won't judge the rest of us by her standards."

"Certainly not," Rayne promised. "I let people prove their worth before I pass judgment. And I think Adelaide proved she isn't worth anything."

The flowers flocking around her all laughed. Zadie introduced her to most of the girls, and she felt a stir-

22

ring of hope that she might make a few friends tonight.

"So, how long are you in England?" Zadie asked as she and Rayne collected champagne from a passing footman.

"A few months. My father is here to buy stock in some steel companies."

"Oh? And your Christmas plans? Will you be staying in London?"

"No, we leave tomorrow by train for Inverness. Lord Fraser has invited us to a party there over the holidays."

"Lord Fraser's estate?" Zadie grinned. "I'm bound there as well. Only we leave in a few days, not tomorrow."

Rayne's heart soared. "You'll be there? Thank heavens, I'll have one friend at least."

Zadie chuckled. "Not to worry. I'll help you survive the end of the season and the holidays."

"Thank you."

"Oh!" Zadie suddenly looked toward a crowd on the opposite end of the ballroom. "I must go, I'm afraid. But I'll see you in Inverness." Zadie gave her a hug and rushed off. It was only as she watched her friend go that she noticed that Adelaide and the other girls nearby were laughing at Zadie.

She heard Adelaide say, "There's only so many ways to change the same old gown before a decent gentleman notices you can't afford a new one."

Rayne drew in a deep breath. If she wasn't careful,

Adelaide might end up with her face drenched in champagne. Lord, Adelaide was testing the strength of her self-control.

Lady Poole plucked her from the wallflowers and sent her onto the dance floor. She had lined up a dozen young men to meet her. In between the twirls and whirls, they talked of her father and her holiday plans. Rayne tried her best to be clever, charming, and entertaining, and she found she wasn't a complete failure.

One man, Devon St. Laurent, teased her mercilessly until she was laughing. He reminded her of the brood of cousins she had at home who all worked for her Uncle Gerard's oil business. Those Egerton boys were delightfully wicked when it came to women, but fiercely protective of her like a little sister.

After an hour had passed, she sought refuge from the dancing in an alcove behind the refreshment table. It was a relief to have a moment alone to gather her thoughts. She'd never been overly fond of crowds. She preferred solitude and quiet study whenever possible. Her father said she was like her mother in that way. Rayne's heart ached at the thought. They had lost her two years before, and her death had left her and her father clinging to one another in shared grief.

She was pulled from her thoughts at the rising sound of Adelaide's hateful gossip.

"I don't know why Lady Poole invited those *dreadful* Americans. They're so..." She lowered her voice to say something to her friends that made them laugh. "I mean, look at her dress. It's more suited to a pigsty. Perhaps that's where she grew up? Slopping her way around with the pigs? And her hair—such a lackluster shade of brown. Her face is quite ugly, don't you think? And those eyes—the color of mud."

That was no private conversation of hushed whispers. The woman had wanted her to hear. Had wanted to hurt her. Rayne bit her lip, holding in tears. Adelaide didn't deserve to see her cry. But she felt so helpless and alone. She needed air; she needed quiet.

She rushed toward the nearest door that led out of Lady Poole's ballroom and grabbed the arm of a passing footman in the darkened corridor.

"Please, is there a library here?"

The young man nodded, and he led her to a room a few doors down.

"Is there anything I can get for you, miss?"

"No, thank you. I just need a moment alone." She slipped into the quiet sanctuary and instantly felt more at peace.

A library was the last place anyone would ever come to in the middle of a ball. It was a trick her mother had used when she first debuted in society and needed a moment alone. It was also how her father and mother had met. They had talked for a full evening and missed the entire ball. It had been love at first sight.

Just thinking of that story brought a smile to her lips and calmed her racing heart. She wiped at her eyes, hiding any evidence of her tears that threatened to cling to her lashes. She shouldn't have let Adelaide get to her, but the girl knew just how to hurt someone like her, where her confidence was at its weakest. At least they would only be here a few months. She could stomach that, couldn't she?

For Father's sake, I must.

The library door opened suddenly, and Rayne spun around, heart pounding. She feared Adelaide had followed her here, meaning to finish what she'd started.

3

A tall, dark-haired man stood framed in the doorway, a dark silhouette against the noise and light from the corridor leading to the ballroom behind him.

He cleared his throat. "My apologies. I thought the room was unoccupied." His voice was pleasant, deep and smooth. It made her think of drinking a glass of brandy and how it made her warm all over. She summoned a polite smile.

"Oh... No, please, I don't mind."

The man hesitated an instant longer before coming inside. As he came into the room, the light from the gas lamps in the corridor outside illuminated him and made her catch her breath. With his intense emerald eyes and handsome face, he looked to be a long-lost prince from some childhood fairy tale her mother used to read. Her eyes moved over his broad shoulders and down to his tapered waist, taking in his tailored but slightly outmoded evening suit just as the strains of a waltz began to play in the distance.

Was this how my mother felt when she first glimpsed my father? A tiny thrill shot through her, like a lightning strike that rippled beneath her skin.

He stared at her for a long moment beneath the hanging oil lamps, and she wondered if it had been a mistake to let him come inside. There was an intensity about him that made her heart race. His green eyes made her think of Zadie, but he was older, perhaps in his thirties, and his features, well... He was striking, if that was the right word to use for a man.

"I could go, if you feel uncomfortable. I just came in here to find a moment of peace," he murmured, his tone all politeness despite the intensity of his green-eyed gaze.

The thought of him leaving, however, left her feeling strangely alone, even though solitude was the reason she had come here. "Please, stay. I suppose it's not at all proper, but..." She didn't finish.

The man chuckled. "I suppose not, but I won't tell a soul if you don't." He took a seat by the fireplace, where flames crackled over logs, and stared into the glowing light.

Rayne waited a moment before joining him. She carefully arranged her skirts and then sat in a second chair not far from his. Being alone with a strange man like this was exciting, a little frightening too. He made no move toward her, nor engaged her in conversation. He simply gazed at the fire as if the flames held the answers he was seeking. The firelight framed his handsome features, casting a melancholy glow about him that warned her he was deep in his own thoughts. She didn't wish to disturb him, so she took the time to study the clear-cut features of his face. Straight nose, noble chin, and a jaw chiseled from marble. He was possibly one of the most handsome men she had ever met.

"Do you find me interesting?" the man suddenly said.

She jolted a little and blushed at being caught in her secret study of him. "I..." She hesitated but then threw caution to the winds. "Yes, you're very interesting to look at. I'm quite sorry." She laughed a little, the sound slightly nervous. She knew it must be rude to admit such a thing, but this man had a way of drawing truths from her, even though they'd only just met.

The man's half-smile only enhanced his charm. "I suppose that's not a bad thing."

"No, indeed," she assured him.

"You're American?" he asked.

She nodded. Her accent was not what one would call fully American, but enough to be noticed. Her mother had sent her to a boarding school when she was younger, which gave her a more transatlantic accent. Her mother had hoped it would make her appeal to more gentlemen in the way of obtaining a suitable match.

"No doubt you needed to escape as well," he said. "Balls can either be wonderful or quite dreadful."

"Dreadful was my case."

"The same for me," the man said. "I wanted tonight to be wonderful, but I failed at that quite spectacularly..." His voice trailed off, his focus locked on the fireplace once again. He didn't finish his thought.

"I understand," she replied quietly. "I find myself flustered when I cannot say or do something, and balls seem to be a most limiting place for a woman."

This caught his attention again. He rested an elbow on the arm of the chair and studied her, his chin in his palm.

"And what is it you wished to say or do tonight that you did not?"

"You'll laugh at me," she warned.

"I may. Does that matter?"

Rayne nibbled her bottom lip, wondering how much she ought to say.

"I wanted to pull the curls off a woman's head and wallop her with a fan."

The man burst out laughing. Rather than be embarrassed, she started laughing as well. "Let me guess—Adelaide Berwick has created yet one more enemy?"

"How did you know?" Rayne demanded.

"That creature is the bane of many a ballroom-goer. She can be merciless and gives no quarter to her victims."

"That does seem to be true," Rayne muttered. She still wanted to pull Adelaide's curls off her head.

"Aside from the challenges Lady Adelaide presented, were you enjoying yourself?" For some reason, she flushed with heat. He still watched her with interest. This man didn't know who she was, didn't know about her father's wealth—they were strangers in the candlelight. A whisper of a thrill stole through her, giving her goosebumps on her arms. He noticed her rub at them.

"Cold?" He removed his coat and moved toward her before she could stop him. He draped the black frock coat around her shoulders. She felt oddly shy as the woodsy scent that clung to the dense woolen cheviot cloth made her feel as though he were holding her, not the coat.

"Better?" He took his seat again, and she glanced down at the blend of fabrics, the dark coat against the vulnerable, pale-rose satin of her ball gown. Something about that, the heavy coat atop her, made her shiver again. The man noticed, but he didn't move from his chair again.

"Forget the ball," he said softly. The rich baritone of his voice pulled her focus to him, as though he'd cast some spell over her.

"Forget?"

"Yes. What would you be doing now if you were not here?"

She fisted her skirts nervously. "Now you truly will laugh at me."

"Honestly, tell me. We have the luck of anonymity between us. No one shall know or laugh at what we speak in this sacred realm of books." He raised a hand. "I vow it upon the sanctuary of the library."

Rayne laughed at his solemn expression, and his responding grin stole her breath. She had never seen anything so beautiful before. She saw the delight in his eyes as he looked at her. Aside from her father, she was unaccustomed to being paid attention to as though she mattered. As an heiress, men saw her as a prize to be won, not a woman to be loved.

"If I could be anywhere..." She thought out the answer carefully. "I think I would've liked to have seen the World's Fair at the Crystal Palace that was here earlier this year."

"Oh?" The man's face brightened. "An explorer of the world, are you?"

She grinned back. "Of sciences and the arts, certainly."

"My grandmother and grandfather attended the fair, or the great Exhibition in 1851. It was in Hyde Park then, before it was moved to Sydenham Hill. It was a city of glass and crystal, according to my grandmother."

Rayne leaned forward in her chair, captivated by him. "What did they love best about the fair?"

"My grandfather was taken with the trophy tele-scope used for viewing the stars."

"The trophy telescope? Why did they call it that?"

"He said it was because the telescope is considered

the trophy of the exhibition, but my grandmother had a far more interesting item in mind." The man's eyes twinkled with mischief.

"More interesting than the telescope?" She couldn't imagine what that might be.

"A diamond captured her eye," he answered in a whisper.

"A diamond? How silly." Rayne laughed. She had no interest in gems or jewels. She was practical and valued knowledge above all else.

The man leaned forward a little, as though sharing the world's most important secret. "The diamond was called the Koh-i-noor, which means *mountain of light*. It is one of the world's largest cut diamonds and now rests in the vault of the Tower of London with the crown jewels. They say it is bad luck to any man who wears it."

"How did the queen acquire it?"

"In the Treaty of Lahore when Britain annexed Punjab in 1849. Ever since, the diamond has courted disaster, and its brilliance has been tainted with blood. Only a female of the royal household is allowed to wear it now." The man continued to speak softly. "My grandmother said it had been bound into an armlet for the queen to wear, with two smaller diamonds flanking it. It rests in a case within black velvet with gas lamps lit around it to make it sparkle. Yet the diamond was flawed and asymmetrical, you see. Prince Albert had it cut for Her Majesty a year after the Great Exhibition, but my grandmother said that day when she saw it, she looked at it head-on, and the uncut gem drew her in like a black cavernous hole, and she said..." The man paused.

"Said what?" Rayne was hanging upon his every word. "Tell me, *please*." She scooted her chair closer to his, until their knees touched.

The man still stared at her, his gaze fathomless as he continued. "She claimed that the diamond showed her half a millennium of bloodshed. Every man who'd held the diamond bore its curse and died. Then my grandmother saw it resting in a crown."

"But is it in the crown now?"

The man shook his head. "No, not yet. It is still in a bracelet that belongs to the queen. I've seen it myself. But I believe my grandmother saw the future."

Rayne gasped. "You've seen it?" Unthinkingly, she reached out to touch his hand on the armrest close to hers.

"Yes. The queen rarely wears the Koh-i-noor. She claims it makes her uneasy, but she still wears it to some state functions. I glimpsed it upon her wrist a few years ago." His gaze grew distant as he seemed to recall the memory. "The way the light glinted off it... I felt like a sailor lured to the rocks by a siren's call. Then I blinked, and the desire to possess it was gone. I felt as though I'd woken from a dark and terrible nightmare."

Rayne's lips parted in shock at the man's fantastic tale, wanting to believe he was teasing her, but she heard the truth in his voice.

"I wish I could've seen it. Not because I like pretty baubles. I do not, but..."

He chuckled. "You have no need of jewels. The beauty of your eyes and the brilliance of your mind are far more attractive than a diamond about your neck."

His frank words startled her. "You think I'm pretty?" Her face flushed, and a happiness blossomed within her in a way that had never happened before when a man praised her looks. Those men had only sought her money, but this man? He had no designs upon her fortune; he was simply looking at her. Longing stirred within her, and she knew for the first time in her life how a lady might easily be compromised by the right man in the right moment...a moment such as this.

"No, not at all," he said flatly. The blossoming hope inside her began to wither. She dropped her gaze, hoping to hide her dismay from him, but he lifted her chin with a finger. "I think you are *stunning*." That rich voice sent wild shivers through her. "*Pretty* is a word for young girls with bows in their hair. *You* are exquisite."

He reached up to trace her gently winged brows and the slightly upward curve of her nose, then slipped his fingers over her cheekbones and down to her chin before resting on her lips. He brushed the pad of his thumb over her mouth, and a dark hunger she'd never experienced before stirred to life. She reacted without thinking, pressing her lips to his thumb and then flicking her tongue against it.

He froze and inhaled sharply. Their eyes locked.

Rayne's stomach started to tumble inside her as she feared she'd let her newfound desire take her too far.

"May I steal a kiss, sweet stranger of mine?" the man asked, his low, hypnotic voice irresistible.

"I've never been kissed before," she admitted. And at that moment she wanted him to be the first. She wanted it more than she'd wanted anything in her entire life.

Her heart stuttered as his eyes darkened with desire. A devilish smile covered his face. There was a possessive look to it, one that said once he began to kiss her, she would beg him never to stop because she would be forever under his spell.

He lifted her easily from the chair and into his lap. Rayne grasped his shoulders, feeling the heat of his body pour into hers. She couldn't resist leaning closer to him.

The man cupped the back of her head, and she leaned into him. They both paused an inch apart, and she savored that building anticipation until his lips touched hers. Her stomach swirled as his warm mouth gently explored hers. It was a kiss of seduction in tender measure. The delicious sensation of their mouths moving together made her blood sing and her head light. Her corset tightened almost painfully as she struggled for breath. She drank in the sweetness of his taste, and a deep-seated need coiled low in her abdomen as he licked at the seam of her lips. She parted her mouth and gasped in shock as his tongue found hers.

The dreamlike intimacy set her heart to trembling anew. Her mind drifted deeper into his kiss. She imagined them seated just like this, her on his lap, a Christmas tree behind them and a kissing bough above them. The man in her dream looked up at her, and in his eyes she saw a future, a life she had never dreamed of before. A potent longing, so intense, made her stiffen in his arms, but she didn't pull away. A sudden fear of losing all this was almost overpowering.

The man held her tight, his kiss intensifying, and Rayne surrendered to the delicious, dark mastery he now held over her body. The fiery possession of his lips sent excitement like she'd never experienced before rippling through her. Her blood pounded, and her knees trembled. She was grateful to be on his lap, clinging to him with everything she had. His hands moved down her body, the heat of his palms seeping through the layers of cloth. A dozen emotions she could barely register whirled around her head as their lips finally, reluctantly separated.

The man was breathing as hard as she was. They both smiled a little shyly as they looked at each other. His eyes roamed over her face, and there was a softness to his expression that made her heart flip in her chest.

"Thank you," he whispered as he grazed the back of his hand against her cheek.

"For what?" Rayne asked.

He was silent a bit longer before he replied. "For showing me what it could have been like."

Confused, she waited for an explanation, but none was forthcoming. The large grandfather clock in the corner struck the late hour.

"We should go before we're missed," he said.

Rayne slipped off his lap, her head a little muddled still from the stranger's drugging kiss. She couldn't find any words as she reluctantly removed his coat from her body and held it out to him. Their hands met as he accepted the woolen frock coat.

"I wish...," the man began, then gave a rueful shake of his head.

"Please... What do you wish?" She had to resist the urge to reach out and touch him again.

"I wish we could have met under different circumstances." The man cupped her chin and leaned down, feathering his lips over hers with one last ghost of a kiss. Then he brushed a finger along her bodice, and she gasped as he plucked a fresh rose from her décolletage and held it up to his nose, breathing in the scent.

"A token. To remember you," he said with a melancholy smile. Then, before she could stop him, he was gone.

Rayne stared at the open doorway, her heart racing with joy and yet strangely painful. Could she fall in love with a stranger and have her heart broken at the same time? There had been some magic at work, something that had drawn them together, and it left her feeling desolate now that he had gone.

She clutched her skirts and tried to calm herself. She

waited a few minutes before returning to the ball. Everything around her seemed the same, yet she had changed. Some great change had indeed begun inside her, something that could not be undone, nor did she wish it to be erased.

If only...

OLIVER HELD THE ROSE BLOOM IN HIS PALM AS HE MET his family on the stairs outside Lady Poole's home. The scent returned him to that memory of the mysterious woman in the library. He would have given anything to drop to one knee and ask her, whoever she was, to be his wife instead of Adelaide. He'd tasted desire on the woman's lips, had glimpsed her keen mind, and had seen a future with her as they'd talked. A future that could not be. Regret clawed a hollow space within his heart as he knew he would never see her again, nor ever know who she was.

He barely listened to his family's chattering as they waited for a hackney to take them to Grosvenor Square. They piled in after one came to a stop, and Everett jostled him with an elbow as he sat down beside Oliver.

"Well, how did it go?"

"Pardon?" Oliver was still replaying that lingering, too perfect kiss. He didn't even know her name, and that was all the better because tonight was all that they could ever have, an exquisite, life-altering kiss.

"What about Adelaide? Did you propose?"

Oliver cradled the rose in his hands as he looked up at the faces of his family. Guilt stabbed at his gut as he realized he'd failed them.

"I didn't. We spoke briefly, and I had every intention of asking her, but..."

"But...?" Everett prompted.

"I needed a minute to clear my head." *And then I met the most enchanting mystery woman in the library.* "And by the time I got back, she'd left."

That woman had changed everything for him. He had found a kindred spirit in her. The connection between them had been intense. He had spoken of cursed diamonds and old memories and lost himself in her eyes.

"Oliver." His mother spoke his name softly, but the concern in her tone caught his attention, pulling it away from the thoughts of the American girl in the pale-pink gown covered with real, blossoming roses.

"Are you holding a rose?" Zadie suddenly asked.

He glanced at his sister and nodded, still clutching the velvet-soft petals of the precious bloom. He had been unable to resist claiming the rose that had featured so prominently above such beautiful breasts. Her breath had quickened as he'd removed the rose from her gown. His desire—yes, desire, not simple lust —had been excruciating, but he had found the courage to walk away as the clock struck midnight, if only because he'd claimed this token of her. Zadie would've teased him for being caught up in a fairy tale or some other nonsense, but the magic in that room had been real. He wouldn't deny it.

"Where did you get it?" Zadie asked, her eyes still focused on the rose.

"I...," he stammered.

"Oliver... Did you take it from Miss Egerton?" There was a strange note of hope in Zadie's voice.

"What? Who?"

"Miss Rayne Egerton, the American. She was at the ball with her father tonight. She wore the most beautiful pale-rose gown with real roses sewn into it." Zadie pointed at the bloom in his palm. "Like that one."

"But what about Adelaide?" their mother interrupted. "Shouldn't we focus on how Oliver will find a chance to offer for her?"

Zadie ignored their mother as she stared at Oliver with a calculating look that bothered him. "You did meet her? Rayne, I mean?"

"We never introduced ourselves. We talked and..." He did not want to admit he'd kissed her as though he might not live to see the dawn in front of his sister and mother.

"Oliver," Zadie said, "Rayne is an *heiress*—far richer than Adelaide."

The occupants of the coach were silent as Zadie's words sank in.

"You mean..." Everett began to chuckle in delight.

"We have someone else to choose from besides old Adelaide? Thank Christ!"

"Everett," Margaret admonished, then turned to Oliver. "Is it true? You met the American heiress tonight? Is she lovely?"

"The loveliest," he assured her, though he was still in shock. His beautiful stranger was an heiress and could be the solution to saving his family and his home. Surely life couldn't be that kind to bless him that way. He buried the sudden guilt at the thought that she might come to hate him if she ever learned how desperate he was to marry her. With Adelaide, she would have known about his situation and understood. Matches for wealth were common, but Rayne? She didn't come from a country that had titles or placed much value on them. He could only hope she'd believe his interest in her was genuine and that he wanted to marry her for more than just her money.

Margaret sighed. "How would we even find her again? These Americans always come and go on a whim, and we are due to leave for Lord Fraser's in a few days."

Zadie beamed in excitement and nudged Oliver. "She will be in attendance at Lord Fraser's house party too. She's taking a train tomorrow afternoon, and I think you should be on it."

"What?" Oliver asked. "My ticket is for three days hence with you."

Zadie shook her head. "No, you need to be alone, and you need to woo her on the train before she arrives at Lord Fraser's. We don't want Adelaide ruining your fortune hunting."

Oliver grimaced at the term. *Fortune hunting.* He didn't want to think of Rayne like that, yet trapping her in a tiny cabin aboard a train to steal a dozen more kisses... That was the sort of hunt he wouldn't mind at all, as long as he could ignore the creeping feeling of guilt about luring Rayne into marriage.

"Do you like her, Oliver?" his mother asked. "Only pursue her if you do. At least with Adelaide we know the kind of person we're dealing with."

His little brother snorted and winked at Oliver. "*Anyone* is better than Adelaide."

"Everett!" Margaret hushed him.

Oliver smiled, feeling hopeful for the first time as he looked at his mother and siblings. "I do. I like her very much."

Now all he had to do was seduce an heiress on a train in two days to save his family and his home. How hard could it be?

4

Rayne peered around at the imposing edifice of King's Cross railway station. Despite the fact that she wore a heavy gown with a black velvet dolman draped over her upper body, she was quite cold, and the breezy station only increased the chill. She stood with her lady's maid, Ellen Moore, a woman in her late thirties whom her father had hired to assist her while they were in England and Scotland. Ellen was quiet but kind and easy to be around, and Rayne felt they were forming a friendship, something she knew was very American, but she didn't care. Ellen passed her a thick black muff to tuck her hands in, and she smiled at her maid gratefully.

"What do you think of it, Ellen?" Rayne pulled her black dolman up around her neck, fighting the chill inside the station. "Quite an architectural marvel, isn't it?"

The maid's eyes roamed over the majestic temple that was King's Cross. It was a beautiful combination of functionality and architectural elegance. Brickwork and ironwork came together to create the vast station. Trains hissed, steam curled up from the tracks, and clouds of white smoke billowed out from the engines. Some people rushed frantically to board cars, while others said tearful goodbyes as they left for the holidays.

Rayne had seen trains before, but the red-and-black steel beasts here were more stately and less fierce than their American counterparts. Several mustached gentlemen in blue uniforms monitored the boarding passengers, checking ticket books and taking luggage when necessary.

"I've never been on a train before," Ellen confessed, her eyes wide. "I've been here plenty of times, but never to travel."

"It's quite fun," Rayne assured her. "The whistle is a little loud if you're close in the first few cars, but I like the motion of it, the vibrations beneath one's feet."

Ellen smiled with mischief. "My mother said that trains used to cause madness in her day."

Rayne and Ellen giggled at the thought. Thirty years ago, trains were fairly new to England, and there had been many silly beliefs that riding upon a train could cause madness and hysteria, especially among women.

"Ladies." Her father rejoined them. "Our train leaves in a quarter of an hour. I suggest we remove ourselves to the first-class refreshment room." Her father escorted them through the crowd to a red doorway with gold letters stating "First Class."

The refreshment room was a large open room with mahogany counters running the length of two walls. Behind the counter, uniformed men waited to serve drinks and sandwiches to passengers. Rayne and Ellen each ordered a glass of lemonade and some cucumber finger sandwiches, while her father purchased a pint of ale and a beef sandwich. Douglas was a fit, handsome man for his age, and it always amused her to see her father tuck away food without it ever adding to his waistline.

"What's our route, Father?" Rayne asked between bites.

He removed a small leather-bound book that had the words *Bradshaw's Monthly Railway Guide* inscribed on the cover and turned to a page he'd marked with a slip of paper.

"We leave London, then journey to Peterborough, which should take three and a half hours. Then we go to Doncaster in two hours. After that, Doncaster to York in an hour. From York to Inverness, it will be about thirteen hours. So we'll have two nights aboard the train."

"What do you think, Ellen?" Rayne asked.

Her lady's maid finished her food with a delighted smile. "I was quite worried when I heard train food was all little gristly cubes and sawdusty sandwiches, but these were marvelous."

Douglas chuckled. "My dear Miss Moore, you're enjoying the benefits of first-class food. I'm told the third-class passengers fare far worse."

"Oh..." Ellen's cheeks were filled with color. "I'm very thankful indeed."

"I do hope our cooks in the dining cabin aren't too terrible. One never knows." Her father finished his ale and checked the time on his gold pocket watch. "Well, we'd best be off."

Rayne, her father, and Ellen left the refreshment room and crossed the bustling station to their train. Rayne paused, searching for a few coins in her reticule as she reached the W. H. Smith stand. The stand contained newspapers and a few books. Rayne purchased a copy of *Jane Eyre* as well as the *Morning Post* before catching up with her father and Ellen. Their luggage had been loaded earlier that morning and would follow them to their final destination. But Ellen and her father carried a few small suitcases to ensure they could change in their cabins for the next couple of days.

They boarded the first-class train car, and Rayne marveled at the expensive wood paneling, which was glossy with black and red paint. The glass windows that framed the cabins for day travel sparkled as she walked along the narrow passage after her father and Ellen.

"Here we are, ladies. Miss Moore, you are here in 6A. Rayne, dear, you are 6C, and I am 6B. I'm told the lavatories are at the end of the hall, and the dining cabin is two train cars behind us." Her father handed them each the keys to their cabins.

"I'll get settled and be right in to help you, Miss Rayne."

"Thank you, Ellen." Rayne entered her own cabin. It had a small bed, perfect for one person, or two people if they slept very close. A tiny closet was opposite the bed, where one could store luggage carried on board.

Rayne removed her dolman and unpinned her hat from her hair and set it aside, then looked down at her gown. It was dark-gray silk bustled gown with black lace that covered her sleeves and hem. Gray was usually such a dull color, but the silk in this gown made it seem almost iridescent. She brushed her fingertips over the silk and closed her eyes as memories of last night stole her focus again.

She had barely been able to sleep after returning from the ball. She had been giddy and at the same time burdened with sorrow, because the man she'd become fascinated by in so short a time was gone, and she would never see him again. She didn't even know his name. Her heart ached at the thought.

Have I missed it? The perfect man and the perfect moment?

Her eyes blurred with treacherous tears. She was not the sort of woman to cry, and this was twice now in two days. Rayne sniffled and reached for the newspaper she had purchased and folded it up for later reading. Then she heard the whistle of the conductor outside, signaling the last few minutes to board the train. She opened her sleeping compartment door to watch the bustle on the platforms and gasped.

A man was rushing across the platform. It was her beautiful stranger from the library! He looked dashing in a dark-blue woolen overcoat lined with dark-gold fur. The heavy braiding of his coat was secured with a series of divet buttons that spoke of his high-born class and good taste in fashion. The man dug into the right side pocket of his coat and pulled out his ticket booklet and showed it to the conductor who allowed him inside the first-class sleeping car. The man removed his top hat and brushed off a dusting of snow, then he glanced around and checked his ticket again before proceeding to the cabin next to hers.

Ducking back into her room just before he could catch sight of her, she closed her door, her breath coming fast and her corset stretched far too tight. He was staying next to her, sleeping one door away. The idea made her flush wildly. What should she do? Introduce herself? No, that was too forward, even for her. Arrange to bump into him in the small confines of the corridor? Maybe.

What are you doing, Rayne? You don't know him. He could be married or engaged, yet you're indulging in romantic thoughts about him?

If he's engaged or married, that's the end of it, isn't it? she countered inside her head. *But what if he isn't?*

She knew she was being very foolish, but something about him made her want to take that risk. That kiss in the library last evening had awoken something inside her, and she didn't want to fall back into the sleep of what her life had been before.

She jumped when someone knocked on her door. She rushed to check her hair and face in the small mirror next to her bed before she answered. Her heart sank as she saw it was Ellen. Of course. Did she honestly expect him to come knocking on her door?

The maid entered her cabin, her eyes looking over Rayne suspiciously as she set down a suitcase of clothes.

"Miss? Are you well? You seem flushed," Ellen observed.

"Oh yes, I'm quite fine."

The train whistle shrieked, and then the train began to move. Ellen gasped and clutched at the wall, muttering about black deviled engines, and Rayne laughed, pulling her down beside her on the bed.

"It takes you a bit of time to adjust. You'll become used to the motion."

Ellen laughed nervously. "I expect it will take a bit of practice to walk while it moves. Your father has gone to the day-travel compartment if you wish to join him and read for a bit." Ellen leaned one hand on the closet door as she stood.

"I might like that, yes." Rayne reached for her books and newspaper. "I shall meet him there in a moment."

Her maid left Rayne to see to her valise and its contents in her closet. When she was done, Rayne gathered her book and newspaper in her arms and exited the cabin. She turned and collided with something—no, someone—and fell back onto the ground.

"Lord, I'm so sorry!" The achingly perfect voice made her look up to see her stranger standing above her.

He had removed his overcoat and was now wearing dark-blue trousers and a gray waistcoat that matched her dress. For some reason the idea of their clothes matching made her giggle. When she covered her mouth in embarrassment, she realized she had spilled her newspaper and dropped her book. He knelt and collected the items as she reached for them at the same time.

Their eyes met, and she saw gentle concern mixed with desire and fascination all at once as he recognized her.

"You... It's *you*," he murmured as he placed the newspaper in her arms and then wrapped his hands around her waist and lifted her to her feet as though she and her voluminous silk gown weighed nothing at all.

"I..." She stared up at him, both speechless and enchanted. He smelled wonderful, like a man who had come in from a snowy landscape outside and brought the scents of winter and man with him. No heavy colognes, no pomades. Just him and the fresh air. It made her a little dizzy with feminine delight, and she wasn't accustomed to that.

"Please, forgive me. I've gone about this like a damned fool." He still held her waist and didn't yet seem to be aware of it. They were standing far too close, and she liked it far too much.

"Shall we start again?" the man asked, and Rayne nodded, her mind and body still focused on his hands around her waist. He seemed unaware of the natural possessive gesture, and she liked it.

Please don't let go, she thought.

"My name is Oliver Conway, Lord Conway."

"Lord? Oh dear, what kind are you?" she asked. He tilted his head in confusion.

"What kind?"

"Lord, what kind of lord? I'm sorry, I'm dreadful at keeping all of the titles straight."

He grinned at her as comprehension dawned on his face. "Viscount Conway."

"Viscount. So above a baron but below a duke?" She nodded to herself. She could remember a viscount. She would have to look up his family in *Debrett's*.

The man chuckled. "*Far* below a duke. Above a baron and below an earl, if that helps." He grinned at her, and it hit her behind her knees, making her feel dizzy with delight.

"I'm Rayne Egerton. No title."

"You were quite the topic of discussion the other night." Oliver gave her a toe-curling smile that made her want to melt into a puddle at his feet.

"You don't mind that I'm American?"

"Why on earth would I mind?"

"Some people do. We're considered brash, bold,

uncouth, and vulgar," she said, rambling on in embarrassment.

"Nonsense. You speak your minds, and you have, for the most part, open hearts. We Brits can be far too closed off and reserved." He still hadn't let go of her, and the feel of his warm hands spanning her waist made her tremble with excitement. His fingers stroked her sides a little, and it would have tickled her if she hadn't been wearing a corset. It felt as though he were playing with her, in the way a man would his sweetheart—the comfortable touches, the little caresses that Rayne had seen others exchange and had always wished to experience herself.

I want to touch him back the same way.

But she couldn't. Instead, she clutched her newspaper and book like a shield, even though she was tempted to drop them again to remove that barrier between them. Her eyes focused on his mouth, a mouth that seemed just as perfect in the afternoon sunlight as it had last night lit by oil lamps and firelight. A mouth that had delivered the most divine kiss.

Oliver Conway. *Lord* Conway. And she was trapped on a train with him. But she was bound for Inverness. What if he got off at Peterborough or Doncaster? How much time did she actually have to be with him?

5

"**W**ill you think me a terrible cad if I admit that I'm glad to have met you again, Rayne?" The man caressed her name in a way that made her body hum. She hadn't given him leave to call her Rayne, but she didn't want him to call her Miss Egerton either. Her given name had never sounded so sensual, so decadent, on anyone else's lips.

"I'm glad too," she admitted as she tilted her head back to look up at him.

"Last night was a memory I had planned to cherish and mourn since I did not believe I would see you again," he murmured. "But it seems fate has other plans for us."

"It does seem that way," Rayne replied, breathless. "Where are you headed now, Lord Conway?"

"Oliver, please," he said. "And I am bound for a Christmas house party in Inverness."

"Are you?" Rayne wanted to jump in excitement. "I am as well. My father and I have been invited by Lord Fraser."

"What a wonderful coincidence!" Oliver finally released her waist, and she instantly missed the connection. "I am Fraser's guest as well." He looked at her newspaper and book. "Are you bound for the day car, by any chance? I was about to go there."

"Yes, I thought I might read for a bit."

"May I join you?" Oliver asked.

Rayne's heart skittered and she nodded, feeling like a girl who'd fallen hard for the first time. And for her it was. She'd never felt under compulsion by a man before, to want to be near him. This was all a new and rather frightening experience.

"Just a moment." He vanished into his cabin and returned a heartbeat later, holding a book of his own. "Lead the way, Miss Egerton."

"Rayne, please, I insist," she replied.

As she started for the day car, she continued to look over her shoulder at him, feeling him close behind. The bustle of her gown flowed between their bodies, whispering against the dark-blue carpets and the wood panels of the narrow passageway. He followed behind her in a slow pursuit that sent her heart racing. He could so easily catch hold of her waist again, hold her against his chest and kiss her neck, her cheek...

The daydream temporarily distracted her as the train clattered and took a turn on the tracks as it departed King's Cross station. She stumbled and had a brief moment to see his face reflected in the window-panes, a handsome god lit by winter sunlight as he dove to catch her.

"Got you," Oliver said as he held her up against the wall until the sway of the train car smoothed out and they were able to walk again.

The feel of his tall, muscled body pressed against hers, pinning her against the corridor wall, had left her breathless in a way that she was beginning to under-stand was dangerous. One of his thighs pressed between the front draping silks of her gown, and even that slight pressure created a low heat deep in her belly.

She tilted her head back to look up at him and smiled, but it faltered as something darker took hold of his features, something wholly masculine that warned her he wanted her, wanted to claim her in the most primal of ways. Every feminine instinct within her quiv-ered at the thought. They were alone here. No one could stop him if he... The thought should have fright-ened her, but it didn't. Part of her wanted Oliver to ruin her in the best way, so much that it created a physical ache between her thighs.

"Are you all right?" he asked.

"Yes..." Her tone was girlishly breathless, but she couldn't help it. He stepped back, and they proceeded on toward the day compartment her father had rented, which was designed for passengers to sit in two rows facing each other. It was perfect to sit and read or converse with fellow passengers, whereas the Pullman sleeping cars were designed just for sleeping.

"Here we are." Oliver reached past, his arm brushing against her bodice as he slid the compartment door open. Then he leaned forward and gestured for Rayne to enter ahead of him.

Her father was seated beside the window, a newspaper in his hands. He folded the paper down to look at her. "Rayne, dear, there you are." He smiled at her, and then his gaze shifted curiously to Oliver behind her.

"Father, this is Viscount Conway. I met him at Lady Poole's ball last night."

"Conway?" Her father stood and held out a hand. "A pleasure, my lord. Please, join us. I'm Douglas Egerton." Her father nodded at the empty seats across from him.

Oliver shook his hand. "Thank you, Mr. Egerton."

Oliver guided Rayne to one of the two empty seats opposite her father. She tried to hide a blush as Oliver's hand lingered on her own before he sat down next to her. Her father watched them curiously before he spoke.

"So, Lord Conway, you are a friend of Lady Poole's?"

"Indeed," Oliver answered. "She and my mother are good friends. My family no longer lives in London, but we made an exception to visit Lady Poole for her ball."

Douglas laughed. "That woman is quite hard to resist. I'm surprised no man has married her yet."

Rayne recalled that Lady Poole's husband had passed away five years ago. "Perhaps she enjoys independence," she suggested. "British ladies have less freedom than we do in America. I wouldn't blame her for choosing freedom to control her fortune and her destiny." She knew she had been too outspoken then by the silence that followed in the train car. Her father didn't mind her speaking out, but he was now studying Oliver, expecting him to react negatively.

"One more thing that makes America quite progressive," Oliver observed with an honest smile. "My mother and sister have often said as much. Of course, the women in my family have always been thinkers and learners. Women of the world, you might say."

Rayne couldn't resist inquiring more about his family. "Women of the world?"

He nodded and leaned back in the black leather seat of their compartment. "My great-grandmother was a duchess and married young at eighteen to my great-grandfather. She was a brilliant businesswoman and kept the dukedom of Essex quite profitable, and she also started an organization that still lives on sixty years later. They call it the Society of Rebellious Ladies."

"Sounds delightful. How does one join?" she asked. If she ever had to remain in London for a longer length of time, she might consider applying for membership.

"I believe you must write an essay on what you believe a woman's place is in society. Station and class do not matter. Duchesses down to scullery maids are welcome, at least according to my sister. I've asked her what they do in the society, but she won't tell me. Something about being sworn to secrecy of a sisterhood."

"Your sister is a member?"

"She is. Zadie is very much like our great-grandmother, or so I'm told."

"Zadie? Zadie is your sister? I met her at Lady Poole's last evening."

His lips twitched. "You've met her?"

"I did." Rayne beamed at him. "She is wonderful. We had a brief moment to share names, but I never learned her surname. Is she traveling with you? I would love to see her again before we reach Lord Fraser's estate."

"She, my mother, and brother Everett are due to leave in three days. I have business with Lord Fraser that sends me north earlier."

"Oh? What sort of business?"

Her father cleared his throat and gave his newspaper a telltale rattle.

"My apologies, Lord Conway, I sometimes forget myself."

"Oliver," he reminded her gently, and she saw no irritation in the green depths of his eyes at her bold questions.

"Oliver," she repeated.

"To answer your question, my family may be leaving our home soon. We may move north to Scotland. Lord Fraser has some opportunities in trade for me that I wish to explore."

"Trade, you say?" Her father set his paper down to look at Oliver again, this time more seriously.

"Yes. Fraser deals with steel companies, and I'm rather interested in that."

"As am I," Douglas affirmed. "Good strong business, steel is. I recommend you invest now and buy stocks. It's a safer bet than railroad stock, yet the prices are building each day. You can double the value of shares in a matter of months."

"Thank you, Mr. Egerton, I will do my best to follow such sound advice," Oliver replied sincerely.

"Where do you currently live?" Rayne asked.

Oliver's mouth quirked up in an amused smile. "North Yorkshire. Do you know it?"

"No, I'm afraid not. I've seen it on maps, of course. It's in northern England. My father said our train will pass through York."

"Indeed we shall. My family lives near West Burton in a place called Astley Court."

"What is North Yorkshire like?"

A fond expression settled on Oliver's face. If he had been a woman, she might've called the look dreamy.

"It is a wild place, the landscapes dramatic, between the haunting moors and the dales. It's a land that had the Romans, Norsemen, and Normans leave their mark on it. In the winter, it can feel like a bleak endless place, and I like the way it feels to stand and look out across the moors. But in the summer, everything blooms or becomes covered in greenery. My brother and I used to run down the banks of the Walden Beck River before we tumbled past forested banks to the edge of Cauldron Falls. Water flows down and to the broken rocks, warming a crystalline pool sheltered by towering stones that make it look like a cauldron."

Rayne almost closed her eyes as she pictured the idyllic setting. "It sounds like you love it there."

"I do," Oliver admitted. "Astley Court, our manor house, has been in my family for two hundred years."

She leaned against the armrest between their two seats. "Then why are you leaving?"

Oliver's green eyes darkened to that of an English forest. "Sometimes one has to let go of the past in order to move forward. The time has come for my family to do the same."

"Oh..." For some reason her heart clenched at the thought of Oliver leaving a place he seemed so clearly to adore. "I'm sorry you have to leave." She reached over to touch his hand, and after a long moment he turned his hand over so their palms met. Then he curled his fingers around hers. Her heart pounded with a strange excitement as Oliver's eyes focused on her lips and she did the same in return. She began to lean into him and only stopped when her father coughed, reminding them both that he was still in the room with them. His paper still concealed his face, perhaps a small sign of his approval—within reason—so she did not pull her hand free of Oliver's, nor did he pull his away.

"What did you bring to read, aside from the paper?" Oliver nodded at the book that lay forgotten on her lap.

"*Jane Eyre*."

"Ah. And what draws you to such a story? The Gothic atmosphere?" He was clearly teasing her, but she couldn't resist proving to him it wasn't only the Gothicness that interested her.

"Actually, I enjoyed the intimate first-person character viewpoint. We see that Jane's moral and spiritual development is colored by psychological intensity. The prose reveals her character through private consciousness as she faces issues regarding class, sexuality, religion, and being a woman in a world dominated by men."

Oliver's eyes twinkled. "Lord, and here I thought it was simply a good read. Those Brontë sisters, one should not be surprised."

"And you? What do you read?" She glanced down at the book in his lap.

He lifted the red-covered book up for her to see.

"*The Black Arrow*?" The shape of a black arrow was printed across the front of the book, as though it had been unleashed by some imaginary bow to land on the cover.

"It's a rather new book. Zadie read it a month ago and thought I might like it."

"What's it about?"

Oliver rubbed his thumb over her hand as he spoke. The intimate little touch thrilled her.

"It occurs during the War of the Roses, with the

Plantagenet line of royalty battling the Tudors, who are usurping the throne. It's the story of a young man named Richard who rescues his lady love, becomes a knight, and avenges his father's murder. He joins a band of outlaws called the Black Arrow."

"That sounds romantic," Rayne sighed. "Like Robin Hood."

"There's nothing better than a tale of outlaws living deep in the English woods." Oliver chuckled. "Would you like to swap? At least until we reach Lord Fraser's?"

Rayne adored the idea, because it guaranteed her having to see him again, and she handed him *Jane Eyre* while she took his copy of *The Black Arrow*.

For the next couple of hours, she and Oliver read in silence, shooting glances at one another every few pages. Oliver would stroke light, teasing touches upon her hand, drawing invisible lines as though he were creating a private map between them. She peeked a few times to see what part he was reading, but when she did so, her skirts spilled over his left leg and their knees touched. When her boot brushed against his, she nearly jerked away, but when he moved his boot closer to hers, rubbing his foot against hers, she thought she might swoon like some Gothic heroine. Never in all of her life had she swooned, and yet here in a train car she was having trouble breathing as excitement gathered within her at each passing touch, each playful caress of his hands or foot. By the time she'd regained her focus, she realized she'd barely read any of the last page she'd been on.

After a while her father yawned, set his paper down, and stretched. Rayne carefully slipped her hand free of Oliver's so as to avoid her father's notice.

"I think I shall retire to my sleeping cabin for a bit," he told Rayne. "It was a pleasure to meet you, Lord Conway. Please join us for dinner tonight in the dining car."

"I'd like that, thank you," Oliver answered.

Now alone in the compartment, a sudden tension filled the room. She shifted, unsettled as she tried to focus on the book. It was rather good, but she was far too distracted by being alone with Oliver.

"For the first time, we begin to understand the wild game we play in life; we begin to understand that the thing once done cannot be undone nor changed by saying I am sorry." Oliver spoke the words she had been reading on the page.

"It is a beautiful passage about regret." She closed the book and tried not to think of the warning that it imparted to her.

"Do you have any regrets, Rayne?" Oliver asked as he set *Jane Eyre* down and cupped her chin, gently making her look at him.

"Regrets?" She hesitated. "A few."

"Name one." He stared at her lips again, and she felt that wild need from the library rise up within her. The need to connect to him in every way, like the moon pulling the tides.

"Letting you leave last night without..."

"Without what?" he asked, seducing her with his gentle deep baritone.

"Without more of this..." She leaned over and kissed him, and then she pulled back, shy and mortified at her forward behavior. But if she hadn't, she might have felt the world freeze beneath her feet forever. Oliver sat back, his eyes unreadable. It had been a mistake to assume that the madness that filled her whenever he was around was shared by him.

"I'm sorry," she whispered. "I shouldn't have done that."

He stood and turned to the compartment door, and she closed her eyes, waiting to hear the door click as he slid it open. Instead, she heard a soft whooshing sound. She opened her eyes and saw he had pulled the blinds down on the compartment, making it completely private. Then he turned back to her. They stared at each other for a long moment.

"A person should do their best to live without regrets," he said, giving her a roguish smile that led to her heart again.

He crooked one finger at her, and she stood, leaning toward him. She was inches away. He wrapped an arm around her waist and tugged her into him. He captured her mouth in a feverish kiss that sent her senses spinning.

He kissed her like a man starved of life and her kiss would bring him back from the brink of death. The corners of her mouth turned up in a delighted grin as she curled her arms around his neck. The raw power of her attraction was astounding, but she didn't question it. He was all she wanted, all she could think about in that moment. He spun their bodies so that he pinned her against the closed compartment door.

"May I touch you?" he asked before he nibbled the soft lobe of her ear.

Rayne let out a tiny whimper of sharp animal need that tore through her. She had to have him touch her.

"Yes. *Lord, yes.*"

He barely stopped kissing her as he slid one hand down between their bodies. Then he curled up the voluminous skirts of her gown and slid his hand beneath them. She gasped as he caressed her inner thighs, and she moaned in shock and delight as he found her center and gently ran a fingertip through her wet folds.

"There... Do you like that?" he asked.

She slanted her mouth over his and raked her nails against the back of his neck. "More...," she demanded. He continued to stroke her, then slid that finger inside her, and she nearly jumped in his arms.

"Easy, love," he chuckled. "Let me show you how good it can feel. Do you trust me?"

"Yes... I do."

She threw her head back as he moved his finger in and out, slow at first, then faster. He used his thumb to brush the small bud of arousal on her mound. Everything seemed to explode around her. She could feel the entire world in that instant. The rumbling of the train upon the tracks, the wind whistling against the compartment windows. She inhaled the scent of Oliver and felt the blood in her veins surging inside her.

A frantic rhythm beat inside her chest. Had she any breath left in her to scream, she would have. But he kissed her again, his tongue sliding inside her mouth, and their mouths moved, mating almost savagely as she drifted down from the trembling perfection of that pleasure he'd created within her. He withdrew his hand, and her gray silk skirts fell back down over her legs. She watched in dazed amazement as he sucked her juices off his fingers before he returned to her mouth for another kiss.

This was a wicked man, with a wicked touch, and Rayne knew she was losing herself to the stranger. His teeth scraped against her neck above the collar of her gown before he returned to her lips and brushed his mouth over hers. Then, finally, he drew back so he could look down at her.

Their breaths mingled in the intimate space of the train compartment, and Rayne knew if he let go of her, she would have trouble walking steadily. He had made her utterly weak-kneed.

"No regrets?" he asked.

She looked into his green eyes and replied without hesitation, "Not one."

"Good." He brushed the back of his hand against her cheek.

"You seem different from last night," Rayne observed.

"I feel different," he said. "Because of you."

"Really? I—"

Someone knocked on the compartment door. "Miss Egerton?" Ellen's voice disrupted them.

"Who's that?" Oliver asked.

"My lady's maid," Rayne nearly groaned.

"You should go to her. We shouldn't be staying too long in here with the shades down," Oliver said.

"I'll go first. Will I see you tonight for dinner?"

"I wouldn't miss it," Oliver promised.

Rayne collected herself and moved a hand over her hair before she exited the compartment and stepped into the hall.

"Time to dress for dinner," Ellen said. "Your father thought I ought to fetch you."

"Thank you, Ellen." Rayne wished the woman could've waited a few more minutes, but Oliver wasn't going anywhere. At least, not yet. They were on the train together and both bound for Inverness.

We have time yet to discover what lies between us.

❧ 6 ❧

Oliver remained in the cabin for a few minutes longer, his heart racing. He licked his lips and smiled. He could still taste Rayne's sweetness there, and it gave him a heady rush. Everett had teased him last evening that the attraction would grow as the size of her fortune did, but Everett was wrong. Rayne was everything Oliver had ever dreamed of having in a wife, and he would have given up everything to be with her. It was simply good fortune that she was also an heiress. A flicker of guilt niggled him at the back of his mind for deceiving Rayne, but he had to ignore it. Rayne had desired him last evening and had been just as interested in him as he had been in her. And they had been complete strangers.

It was more than her beauty that drew him to her. Rayne was real and tangible to him in a way that other young ladies didn't seem to be. They presented a facade of what they *should* be instead of simply being who they were. Rayne had no such pretensions. It was as if he could reach out and touch her soft satin skin and feel her dreams through that simple connection alone.

Oliver smiled as he retrieved his copy of *The Black Arrow* from where she had forgotten it among the newspaper pages scattered on the seat. He stroked the book's spine and in his mind relived the sweet moment when he had her pinned against the door of the compartment. He had almost come undone himself as her face had revealed that intimate look of a woman in the throes of passion. There was nothing more beautiful than the way her lashes had fluttered or the way a heavy blush had stained her cheeks. He had wondered then what beauty there would be in seeing the rest of her flushed like that when she lay beneath him in a bed.

He took a long moment to let his ardor cool before he took his book and returned to his own cabin in the sleeping car. Dinner was in an hour, and he needed time to prepare. He had barely made it to the train on time. It had taken longer than he thought to have his ticket changed, and then he'd had to meet with the officers in charge of luggage. He had only a few days of clothes, and they would have to do until he reached Inverness.

As he reached the cabin, he heard feminine voices coming from next door and grinned. He'd paid another man on the platform almost twice the cost of the ticket to ensure that his cabin was next to Rayne's.

Oliver slipped into his cabin and then removed his valise from the closet and set it on the bed so he could retrieve his evening clothes. His valet, Benjamin, would catch up with him at Lord Fraser's in two days, but thankfully he had no need of him today. He donned his black trousers, which were cut narrower than his usual trousers and finished with black braid on the seam. Then he donned a lounge jacket that fell to his hips. It would be more suitable for dinner on a train than a coat and tails. No doubt Mr. Egerton would be sporting a tuxedo, which was all the rage in America at the moment. The British, however, were reluctant to embrace the look. Oliver knew his dinner jacket would be an appropriate compromise between the two dueling fashion trends.

He brushed his coat with the suit brush and carefully checked his appearance in the small mirror. He had only a handful of days to get Rayne to fall in love with him. A more cynical or mercenary mind might be focused on seducing her or trying to compromise her into marriage, but that was not his intention. He wanted Rayne to love him so that when he proposed she would be happy with him and not resent him for marrying her for her fortune. If he played the hand of cards he had been dealt in the right manner, Rayne would not care about his lack of fortune because she would love him, and he would endeavor to make her happy. Still...he couldn't quite shake the small dark cloud forming in the back of his mind that whispered he was going to hurt her when she discovered the truth. That was why he had to make her fall in love with him.

Though it was too soon for him to believe he loved her, she had captivated him with her mind and her body, and he truly believed his heart would pose little resistance in the days to come.

He opened the door to his cabin and stepped into the hall. Through the windows, he saw that the sun had set behind the distant hills, but the train would roll on through the night. They had left Peterborough one hour ago, and now the train was headed toward Doncaster and would pass through York overnight.

"Lord Conway?" The voice stopped him dead in his tracks. He spun to see a woman in a mauve evening gown. He stared at the woman, worry prodding his stomach at this unforeseen complication.

"Ellen? What are you doing here?"

Ellen Moore stared back at him in confusion. "I am accompanying my new employer to Scotland. And you, my lord?"

"Your new employer?" The dread forming in his stomach grew. "You wouldn't happen to be working for the Egertons, would you?"

She nodded.

"Christ," he muttered. "Come in here." He gestured to his cabin.

Ellen hastily followed him inside, and he closed the door. Then he faced Ellen, one of the women he'd had to let go from employment in his own home only two months before.

"How is Miss Conway?" Ellen inquired hopefully.

"She is well, but she misses you," Oliver said.

Ellen had been Zadie's lady's maid for three years, but due to their situation, Oliver had been forced to let go of half of his staff. He and Everett now shared a valet, and Zadie shared a lady's maid with their mother. Oliver had done his best to provide sufficient funds to let every servant have a chance to get by until they found new work.

"Thank you again for the references. It helped me obtain my position," Ellen said with a sad smile. "The Egertons are lovely people, especially Miss Egerton."

"I'm glad to hear it." Oliver hesitated. "Ellen, I must beg a matter of secrecy with you. Regarding my family's...situation."

Ellen's brows rose, then narrowed. "My lord, I would never speak untoward about you, but why are you so concerned?"

"Well, you see, I am attempting to court Miss Egerton. We met last night, and I'm quite taken with her." He would not say he was fortune hunting. He refused to call it that.

However, the lady's maid's shrewd gaze confirmed she had already made the connection. "You wish to..."

"Marry Miss Egerton."

"For her fortune—"

"Not entirely," he cut in. "Because I genuinely like her. I met her last night before I knew she was an heiress, and now, well, perhaps fate has a kindness planned for my family after all."

"Lord Conway, you know how much affection I have for your family, but surely there is another way?"

"There isn't. I went to see the banker in charge of our loans, and he could not give us any more extensions. I had been about to propose to Lady Adelaide when I met your Miss Egerton."

Ellen's face pinched. "Oh my lord, not her. She's the worst sort of creature. It would devastate Miss Zadie."

"It would indeed, but she is my only other choice. Please, Ellen, I beg you. I find myself faced with a horrible choice: an honest transaction with a woman I cannot love, or a chance at happiness that requires me to be dishonest for a time. It is not a quandary I take lightly. I don't wish to start a marriage out like this, it galls me to even think of hurting Rayne by hiding my financial state."

Ellen crossed her arms, eyeing him with a severity that was wholly inappropriate given their stations and yet richly deserved under the circumstances. "You truly like Miss Egerton?"

"I do," he promised. "She bewitched me last night long before I even knew her name."

"Then I will keep your secret, my lord, but you must win her on your own. You will have no help from me, not because I don't wish you well, but because she deserves a man who will value her as a person, not as an heiress. That is my only advice. Truly win her heart, my lord. She deserves to have a marriage based on trust and love, she shouldn't have to worry over whether you married her for herself or her money."

He'd managed to avoid feeling guilty about his motives for seducing Rayne until now, but Ellen had reminded him that what he was doing was what all fortune hunters did. But unlike those callous individuals, he wanted to love Rayne, wanted to be married to her not just for the money. Surely that mattered.

"I've always liked you and your family, my lord, but I know that desperation can turn even the sweetest fruit sour. If I come to believe your intentions are anything other than what you say, I will tell Miss Egerton the truth."

"That is fair, and I would expect nothing less from the woman who kept my dear sister away from more than one cad in her time." He opened his cabin door and let her slip into the hall, then made his own way a moment later.

As he stepped into the dining car, his heart stopped at the sight of Rayne. Her beauty was intoxicating, and he felt he could become drunk on the sight of her alone. She looked exquisite in a blue-and-pink plaid silk evening dress. Pale-blue three-quarter-length sleeves matched the pale-blue revers that separated the bustle from the front skirts, which were draped with pale-cream lace. She was a picture of perfection, as delicious looking as a dessert sitting in a confectioner's shop window. She turned, the pleated train trailing behind her as she laughed at something her father said.

He hadn't heard her laugh before, and he liked it more than he could say. She swayed as she walked farther down the dining car on her father's arm, and a bittersweet ache settled in Oliver's chest.

Ellen stepped in behind them, and the three of them proceeded to a set of tables. Oliver hurried to catch up with them.

"Oh, Lord Conway, it seems the dining car has only two tables left, each seating two. I don't suppose you would prefer to dine with Rayne tonight? I'm sure she's quite tired of listening to me talk and would love a charming younger dinner companion."

Rayne chuckled. "You know that isn't true, Father." Oliver didn't miss the fond look she sent her father's way. It was clear they were very close, and Oliver liked that, even though he knew it would make it more difficult for him to win the older man's trust.

Mr. Egerton's eyes twinkled. "Perhaps not, but I do think you would enjoy someone new to talk to. I would be happy to dine with Miss Moore."

"Thank you, Mr. Egerton. I would be delighted." Oliver couldn't believe his luck. Rayne's father must have sensed that Rayne and he had a liking for each other and possibly approved, at least so far as to allow them time to converse at dinner.

Oliver saw the pair of open tables, which were across the aisle from each other. He offered Rayne his arm and relished the blush on her face as she slipped her hand in the crook of his elbow as he led her to their table. He pulled her chair back for her as she took her seat and then sat across from her.

"You look magnificent," he said softly.

She looked down, clearly embarrassed. "Thank you. I don't normally wear such gowns, but Father ordered them from Paris, and, well, it has been fun to wear them."

"What do you normally wear?" he asked.

"I do love a nice gown, but they tend to be a tad more practical," she reflected with a small smile, as though amused at the admission. "I work at my father's office a few days each week, and it is easier that way."

"You work with your father?" That startled him, though he didn't disapprove.

"I do. Most men find that unattractive, or at least inappropriate." She said this a little coolly, as if he was being tested. Well, luckily for her, he believed she would like his honest view on the matter.

"I find that very appealing. Idleness is nonsense in my opinion. Men and women alike are creatures who like to be busy, to be useful, to be innovative. What use are we to our fellow man if we do nothing to contribute? I know that sounds odd coming from a member of the landed gentry, but I have never believed that I should sit by and let others work while I do nothing but reap the benefits."

A waiter approached their table and poured them each a glass of wine. Rayne reached for hers. "So you don't mind a woman who works?"

"I do not," he promised. "As a son and brother to two very intelligent, driven, passionate ladies, I see only strength in women."

Rayne relaxed a little, and he knew he had won an important battle tonight.

"Tell me, what sort of work do you do?"

She laughed. "My father calls me an office manager. But it is more a mix of accounting, invoice collections, and correspondence with investors and clients."

"Incredible." Oliver meant it. Those qualities would make for a masterful mistress of Astley Court. Running an estate took skill, patience, and determination.

"I'm glad you think so," she admitted, that shyness now back in her eyes.

"As my sister often reminds me, it should not matter one whit what a man thinks."

She giggled. "All the same, I'm glad."

"Rayne..." He spoke her name softly. "Given last night and this afternoon, I am finding myself growing attached to you. May I..." He paused, wondering if now was the right time to ask or if he was rushing it. But then he mustered his courage and continued. "May I court you?"

"Court me?" she echoed in a surprised whisper.

"Yes. If you are not interested, I understand, but—"

"Yes." She cut him off, which made them both laugh at her eagerness.

"Yes?"

She nodded, a blush staining her cheeks, and then she took a large sip of her wine.

"Good, then let us learn more about one another," he said.

"How do you propose to do that?"

"We shall play a question game. You ask me a question, then I ask you."

She sipped her wine, studying him intently, and he wondered what sort of question she was brewing up.

"How do you take your tea?" She looked at him so seriously, he wanted to laugh again.

"A most penetrating question. A touch of cream, no sugar," he replied. "My turn. Favorite color?"

"Green."

"A sensible choice. Any particular shade?"

"The color of your eyes," she blurted, then covered her mouth.

He couldn't resist smiling. "Until yesterday I favored red, but now I'm bewitched by the color of *your* eyes. They are an enchanting shade, a diamond blue-gray." He meant it. Nothing he said or would ever say to her would be false. He needed to win Rayne's heart along with her hand, and he would not lie to her to do so.

"I dreamed about cursed diamonds last night,"

Rayne said in a scandalized whisper. Her eyes, so deep and clear, were full of longing and desire.

"Is that *all* you dreamed about?" he said conspiratorially as the waiter set plates of quail and potatoes in front of them.

"Perhaps. Perhaps not," Rayne replied with an impish smile. He nearly choked on his wine when she gave him a wink.

"I think I adore you," he whispered, and she blushed.

She was a fascinating contradiction of a woman. Clearly passionate, but shy about expressing it, except when she wasn't. Given how society treated such things, he couldn't blame her for being inconsistent in her expressions. More likely than not, she was passionate and outspoken by nature, but society was continually reinforcing that a woman must be quiet and meek. He much preferred the former in a woman and not the latter.

"I'm not usually this forward, at least in regard to romance," she whispered back. They were both aware of how close the other diners in the first-class dining car were, and the fact that their conversation could be overheard. It was frustrating and exciting at the same time.

"Neither am I," he added. At least, he hadn't been in the last few years. He had put his days of roguish behavior behind him, but this woman seemed to draw that old devil out. If he wasn't careful, he would be seeking an invitation to her cabin tonight, and it was far too soon for that.

"I confess, I don't seem to be sensible around you," she said.

"I feel a bit wild myself. Perhaps that's a sign of something?"

"Perhaps it is simply lust at first sight?" Rayne asked, still lowering her voice as they ate their way through the first course.

"Lust, yes, but a desire that runs deeper as well, I hope." He was quiet a long moment. "Tell me about your home, your family."

Rayne's eyes darkened to a stormy color that made him think of spring rain.

"My mother passed away two years ago. My father was madly in love with her. I became more involved in his company to help him with his grief."

He knew what it meant to care for a parent who had lost their spouse. But unlike Rayne, he'd had the good fortune of sharing that burden with his siblings.

"And who helped you? Losing one's parent is a difficult blow to one's heart."

"No one, really. I'm strong enough to bear it." But her eyes said otherwise. They became downcast, and her eyes began to shimmer. Rayne had taken her father's grief and carried it along with her own. That alone told him how strong she was, and he wanted to be the man who helped her carry those burdens from now on.

Oliver reached across the table to catch hold of her hand, forgetting that they were not alone.

"There is nothing wrong with relying on someone when you are hurting."

She didn't pull her hand away; she simply shrugged. "There isn't anyone to rely on."

He squeezed her hand gently, hoping she could hear his silent vow. *There will be, if you let me.*

When the waiter delivered two plates of blancmange for dessert, their hands separated. The milky white pudding was shaped into an artful mold surrounded by thinly sliced strawberries. Oliver watched Rayne dip her dessert fork into the blancmange and take an experimental bite. Her face lit with a glowing pleasure that stole his breath.

"I say, Rayne, this is rather good," Mr. Egerton said from across the aisle. Oliver was dragged back into the awareness that he and Rayne were not alone. It was so easy to forget that when he was with her.

"Yes, it is good," Rayne replied to her father. He nodded and returned to his meal.

"Tell me about your home," Oliver asked, hoping she would have happy memories to share.

"Home is... Well, not exactly a place for me anymore. My father's business has always kept us in New York, but that city never felt like home. I had no idyllic place to explore as a child, no enchanting waterfalls, no dusty old attics, no place to call my own."

"It's never too late to find one's home." He imagined

she would fall in love with a place like Astley Court and quickly make it her home.

"It would be nice to have a place like yours," she said, seeming to read his thoughts.

"Perhaps you can. I would love to extend an invitation to you and your father to stay with us after Christmas." He hoped that she would be wed to him before then, but he couldn't wager on that.

"I would like that. I will ask my father this evening."

"Ask me what?" Mr. Egerton and Miss Moore had finished their dinner and had risen from their table.

"Lord Conway has invited us to stay at his house, Astley Court in Yorkshire, when we are finished with our visit to Lord Fraser's."

"Thank you for the invitation, Lord Conway. We would be delighted to accept." Douglas offered him a smile, but Oliver could see the man was appraising him. Perhaps he had overheard more of their conversation than he was letting on?

"Ladies, forgive me, I'm going to steal Lord Conway for a glass of brandy."

It was as Oliver suspected. Douglas was aware of Oliver's interest in his daughter, and now he would begin the interrogation.

"Oh..." Rayne sighed in obvious disappointment.

"Breakfast tomorrow?" Oliver volunteered, and she brightened again.

"Yes, that would be lovely." She rose from the table,

and she and Miss Moore headed in the direction of the Pullman sleeping car.

"This way, Lord Conway," Douglas Egerton said.

Oliver knew this might well be the hardest battle for Rayne's heart. He did not wish to lose her because of her father's disapproval. He cast one last look at Rayne's retreating figure, and it gave him the strength to face her father.

I must win them both.

7

Oliver sat down across from Mr. Egerton at the back of the dining car as a waiter brought them two glasses of brandy. He tried to remain calm, but damned if he wasn't a bit nervous. The atmosphere between him and Rayne's father had grown a bit cold, just enough to give him a slight worry as to what was to come.

"Well, I'm not one to beat around the bush, waiting to see what rushes out. Let's get to the heart of the matter. You are interested in my daughter, Lord Conway." It wasn't a question.

"I am, Mr. Egerton. She has consented to my courtship."

"And what about me? Do you care to ask me if I consent?" Douglas wasn't angry, but there was a gleam in the man's eyes that would have made Oliver nervous if he had been a younger man. But far too much was at stake for Oliver to be afraid.

"I am of two minds on that matter," he said diplomatically. "Rayne is a woman possessed of her own mind and desires and believes she does not need any man's approval for the choices in her life. I respect that. But at the same time, I do seek your approval for my suit toward her. I respect a father's need to look out for the best interests of his child. My intention was to come to you if Rayne and I decided to marry. But we have only begun our courtship, so I thought it imprudent to assume such an outcome was guaranteed."

Douglas sipped his brandy, remaining silent long enough that Oliver assumed the man was still testing him.

"How did you meet my daughter last night? I did not see her dance with you."

A clever *and* observant father. Oliver liked him far too much for that, even though it made seducing Rayne more difficult.

"We both sought refuge from the ball in Lady Poole's library. We met and conversed for a short while but did not exchange names. I did not think I would see her again, but she made quite an impression on me."

"The library?" Douglas's eyes softened. "Libraries are wonderful places, aren't they? I met her mother in a library. Jeanette was never one for crowds, and Rayne is a little like her mother in that regard."

"Rayne said she passed away two years ago. My condolences on your loss."

Douglas's gaze grew distant. "Thank you. No one prepares a man for losing a woman he loves with all his heart. It felt as though my own heart was ripped out and cast into a raging fire. Rayne is all I have left of her."

Oliver met his gaze and saw a flicker of pain there. "My father passed over a year ago. I wondered at times if perhaps he would come back to haunt me. We have such strong stories of hauntings here in England, but my mother told me something that put my heart at ease. She said the world has its ghosts, but they are not the phantoms we imagine drifting among the graveyard stones. She said the spirits of those we love never truly leave us. Once a soul is born, it can never perish—it merely changes form. She told me that my father's eyes were those of my own, that his laugh can be heard in my brother's voice, and his honest and loving heart beats within my little sister's chest. When my mother looks upon us, she sees the separate pieces of her husband, as though he were one being again."

Rayne's father gave a bittersweet smile. "My Jeanette is certainly within Rayne. It makes it hard for a man to let go."

Oliver knew what he meant. It would be hard to let go of Rayne because she would marry a man and live her own life far away from her father.

"If she married the right man, you need not ever

lose her," Oliver said, hoping he would understand that he would be a welcome member of the sometimes-boisterous Conway clan.

"And are you that man, Lord Conway? If you aren't, then you would be wise to leave my daughter alone before she becomes too attached."

The gauntlet has been thrown, Oliver thought.

"I would like to be that man. As a peer of the realm—"

"Titles mean little to me. I value a man's actions." Douglas threw back his brandy in one gulp. "Court my daughter if you wish, but if you break her heart..." Douglas fixed him with a powerful stare. The unspoken threat was nevertheless made abundantly clear to him.

"I shall heed your warning, Mr. Egerton." Oliver finished his brandy. "I will retire now."

He bid Douglas good night and returned to his sleeping cabin. He listened next door but heard no sounds coming from Rayne's cabin. It was hard to hear much given the sounds of the train. As he prepared for bed, he changed into his dark-blue jacquard silk dressing gown. As he was fastening the sash around his waist, someone knocked at his door.

As the night steward had not yet come by to check the oil in the lamp in his cabin, he assumed that was who was there. Oliver opened the door.

"Good of you to come, my lamp is low—" His words died as he saw Rayne standing in her nightgown with a gold-and-black dressing gown over it. It made her look like a beautiful red admiral butterfly with the puffed sleeves near her shoulders. Her hair was loosely bound at the nape of her neck by a black ribbon, and she'd pulled her hair over her shoulder so it tumbled down in a riot of brown waves.

"May I come in for a moment?" she asked.

His mouth was too dry to form words as he stepped back to allow her entrance. Then he closed the door. The woman was far too lovely for him to keep his wits about when she was around.

"Did anyone see you?" he asked.

"No, the steward has extinguished all the lamps except the ones in the passageway between the train cars. I waited until he was gone."

"Good, I wouldn't want to cause any scandals," he said.

Rayne flashed that impish smile at him. "The scandal might be worth it."

Oliver almost laughed. He was supposed to be the heartless fortune hunter, and yet the little American heiress was the one sneaking into his cabin dressed so enticingly. It would be so easy to peel the dressing gown off her body and remove the filmy white peignoir she wore under it. And her body, with its luscious curves, would no doubt erase the last bit of his frayed control.

"I realize how silly this is," Rayne said as she reached up to hold her dressing gown closed. "But...I didn't want the night to be over."

The sweetness of her sentiment stunned him. She

was impossibly innocent, yet not naïve. She'd sought him out because her heart called to his. The need to not be apart from him must have been overwhelming. He felt it too, that strange and wonderful pull toward her like he'd never felt for any woman in his life.

"I feel the same, so perhaps we are silly together." He gestured to his bed. "Come and sit. We shall talk."

He sat down opposite her in the small armchair beside his bed.

"What were you like as a boy?" she asked.

"Me?"

She nodded, excitement filling her eyes. Oliver couldn't resist laughing as he considered his answer. "Trouble. Certainly trouble. I was forever escaping the house to avoid my schooling. Once Everett was old enough, we would sneak out together to go into the woods and set snares for rabbits, or we'd go fishing in the river."

Rayne laughed at this, clearly delighted in his penchant for mischief. It made him all the more curious about her.

"And what was a young Rayne like?"

She looked down at her black silk slippers. "Trouble. Certainly trouble."

Oliver chortled. "You? Trouble? I cannot picture it."

"You should," she insisted with a mischievous smirk. "I was quite clever escaping my house as well, only I would go down to the stables and ride my pony. When I was older, I tried to go to my boarding school without my corsets. I may have burned one or two in protest."

"You burned a corset? Why?"

"Because they're impossible to breathe in most of the time. You become even a little bit excited and *poof*!" She made a gesture with her hands to show she was falling. "You faint dead away. It's no wonder men believe we're so delicate. If we were allowed to breathe normally, we'd be quite different during the day, I assure you."

"Surely you don't wear them *all* the time. I know that during afternoon teas, ladies do not wear corsets—it's why we men aren't allowed to attend those teas." Oliver knew women wore them most of the day, but he was curious to see what she would say.

"We don't wear them all the time. I'm not wearing one *now*."

"Dear God, woman, are you trying to kill me?" He was seconds away from creating the very scandal he wished to avoid.

Rayne left his bed and came over to him and settled herself on his lap. She kissed him, her small delicate hands framing his face. He gave up fighting his desires then. He had never been a saint, and he wasn't about to become one now.

A SMALL PART OF RAYNE TRIED TO WARN HERSELF

that this wild, reckless behavior was a bad idea, but the rest of her was blissfully lost in kissing Oliver. When he had opened the door and she'd seen him wearing those silk sleeping trousers and his lounge jacket, she'd been both stunned and aroused. Something about Oliver in a state of undress made him twice as irresistible. Perhaps it was that the veneer of being a gentleman was gone and in its place was a man of flesh and blood, one of dark carnal desires. That was the Oliver she wanted now.

He cupped her face as he slowed their fevered kisses to look at her. She tried to catch her breath.

"Are you all right?" he asked as he stroked her bottom lip. "I'm not scaring you?"

She shook her head and licked her lips. "I came to you," she reminded him. She curled her arms around him and played with the strands of hair at the base of his neck.

"I know, and as much as I am enjoying this, love, I don't want you to think that I have expectations."

"But you have desires, I hope?" she asked. A sudden fear that she was the only one truly feeling this way made her draw back a little.

"Oh, I do. Great, *hungry* desires." His eyes turned dark, and she saw what she was hoping to see, that he was barely in control of himself.

"Could we...stay together tonight, just to sleep? I don't think I'm ready yet for..." It was hard to explain why, even to herself, but she wanted to lie beside him tonight and feel his heartbeat against her cheek and listen to the rhythm of his breath. Her mother used to say that people showed who they really were when they were asleep. If a frown marred their brow, worries troubled them; if they smiled slightly, their dreams were as sunny as their disposition. She wished to know what Oliver was like at his most vulnerable.

He groaned approvingly at her scandalous request and twined his fingers in the hair that spilled down her shoulders. "Of course."

She leaned in to press her forehead against his. "But...I would like a bit more of this first..." She pressed her mouth to his and delighted in tasting his laughter before he conquered her lips with his own.

Oliver Conway was indeed a master of kisses. He knew when to flick his tongue against hers, when to deepen the kiss, and when to pause and let her regain her breath. He held her full attention just with the power of his lips. She couldn't imagine what he would be capable of if he used the rest of his body on her.

She shivered with longing and pressed closer against him. It was strange and comforting to feel the train clacking along on the tracks beneath them. The sound was hypnotic and kept her bound in this perfect moment where she and Oliver had nothing but their endless kisses together. When the train came to a stop, she looked around in confusion. A distant whistle shrilled in the night.

"Doncaster," Oliver murmured before he nibbled

her earlobe, and her body was once again under his magnetic thrall. Soon enough the train started moving again, and she knew they would be on their way to York next. York, where Oliver lived. She recalled his face as he'd mentioned having to leave his home behind, and it saddened her. Her heart ached, and her sorrow for him bled into her kisses. He seemed to sense her emotions as he pulled her closer, the embrace more comforting now than sensual.

When their mouths parted, he drew in a deep breath, and she saw his sensual expression fade a little.

"Are you tired yet?" he asked.

"Not quite... We could play cards and talk? That is, if you have some?"

"I do." He let her slide off his lap and went to retrieve a deck from his suitcase. "A gentleman never leaves home without a deck of cards." He looked at her with a wolfish smile. "Or a good book."

"It's rather nice to meet a man who reads. Most gentlemen I've been introduced to lately don't seem to know that books exist anymore. It's all horse racing or stock markets when we talk."

Oliver smiled, the expression confident and tinged with amusement. "You've been meeting all the wrong men. A good Cambridge man always reads. It's those Oxford bastards who don't."

She couldn't help but laugh. She'd heard more than once of the long-standing rivalry between the two elite British universities.

He slipped the cards from their box and began to shuffle them in his hands with the flair of a man who knew his way around a deck.

"You know how to play Bread and Honey?" he asked.

"I think so. I played once or twice. You deal all the cards one at a time facedown. And there are cards called blackbirds that determine what each of us can play following the reveal of a blackbird card so that we can gain more cards in our respective stacks?"

"Yes, exactly. The winner is whoever ends up with the most cards."

They sat down on the floor beside the bed, and Oliver deftly dealt the cards between them. Over the next hour, Rayne laughed as she and Oliver played. They talked about themselves, in between his teasing about her spectacular ability to lose the game, and she clung to the details of his life, how he had served for a time aboard a naval ship when he was in his twenties.

"It was the only real fight my father and I ever had," Oliver said as he turned over another card. "I thought at the time that he was trying to control me since I was the eldest son and heir, but as I grew older and wiser, I realized he was afraid that I might be injured or killed."

"Fathers can be like that. They want to protect you, but they don't realize you need to live your own life, make your own mistakes." Rayne thought of how her own father never tried to control her, but he had made it clear that he would not let her marry just anyone.

Her inheritance as his only child put her in a clear position to become wealthy beyond most men in America. They'd had many discussions about fortune hunters and the danger of being alone with men. Rayne wasn't naïve. She knew a man could compromise a woman and attempt to force a marriage. But she wanted love, wanted to find a man who would love her for herself, even if she was as poor as a church mouse. But how did one find a man like that?

Perhaps in a library?

That was why she'd been so attracted to Oliver. He'd had no idea who she was, and yet he'd liked her. Even now, he seemed unconcerned with her wealth, whereas most gentlemen would have pressed her with questions regarding her father's business, which always led to talk of money. She felt she could trust him too, in a way she hadn't been able to trust any other men, aside from her father.

Rayne focused back on the card game and cursed as Oliver won the game by turning over his final card and adding it to his larger stack.

"Damn!" Rayne tossed her remaining cards down. "You have an unfair advantage."

"Suppose I do. I've been playing Bread and Honey since I was a child."

"See, advantage!" she teased and leaned back against the edge of his bed. She yawned, and then heat rushed to her face in embarrassment. Her mother used to remind her that it was rude to yawn in the presence of others.

"Tired?" Oliver's face was gentle with a hint of amusement, and her embarrassment faded.

"I am now." She had been so nervous coming here tonight, but, as always, being with Oliver was impossibly easy.

In some ways, it felt as though they'd been together for years, playing cards until after dark and whispering about their lives as the oil in the lamp burned low. Her heart quivered with a desire for it to always be like this, to have Oliver as a husband and...to have a life together with him.

He gathered up the cards and returned them to his suitcase before he pulled back the sheets of his narrow bed in silent invitation.

Rayne stood and removed the black-and-gold dressing gown she wore and stepped out of her satin slippers before she climbed in. Oliver watched her a long moment, allowing it to build with delicious tension before he removed his lounge coat and revealed his bare chest. She was left in a daze at the way the light from the lamp made his skin look soft and golden. He had a patch of dark hair at the top center of his chest and a trail of dark hair that started a few inches below his navel. Her gaze followed it down to the waistband of his satin sleep trousers. She swallowed hard as it became all too real. She was alone in a man's sleeping cabin. Alone in his bed.

Oliver extinguished the oil lamp, and darkness swallowed them up. Her heart hammered wildly against her ribs as he joined her in bed, but it eased as Oliver pressed his body against hers and slowly relaxed. The heat of his bare upper body soothed her, and she pressed her cheek against his chest. The beating of his heart was so steady that she could set a pocket watch to it.

After a moment, he reached to touch her hair, stroking it gently. That was how she knew she was lost to him. He was a blend of gentleness and fierce passion, and he cared about his family and his home. He didn't have a problem with a woman who worked or liked to learn about business. He was perfect—*too* perfect.

A sudden flicker of doubt was there. Could this be an act? Was he like the others?

Those men in dashing suits who brought flowers and gifts to her door, all in an attempt to woo her, to take her fortune and leave her brokenhearted? If that was the case, then he was the most clever one yet, because she was falling for him. He'd only been a gentleman with her thus far and had done his best to keep her from being compromised. Any other fortune hunter would have had witnesses ready in the library or in the day compartment to see them kissing and expose them to try to force a marriage, but that hadn't happened with Oliver.

He must be different. He must be...

❦ 8 ❦

Morning arrived with sweet, slow awareness. Rayne had forgotten sometime during the night that she had come to Oliver's cabin and stayed there in his arms. As it came back to her, she felt her body nestled against his, and she almost giggled in delight at her own wicked behavior. What would those stodgy ladies in the Knickerbocker Club back in New York think of her?

Oliver lay on his back, one arm folded behind his head as he slept. She rested her chin on his chest and studied him. A night beard shadowed his jaw, making him so very human, so very masculine, and so very real in that moment. She reached up and traced her fingers over his jaw, feeling the slight scrape of stubble beneath her skin. The touch was so intimate, like something only a lover or a wife might do. Rayne was filled with a desire then to be Oliver's lover, to be his wife. She still knew so little of him, but she knew more about him than many people who got married.

He shifted beneath her touch, turning his face toward her hand and pressing a kiss to her fingers. Then he opened his eyes, and his slumberous expression toward her was incredibly intimate.

"Did you sleep well?" he murmured.

"Yes. You?" she whispered, not that anyone could hear them, given the train's noise.

"Wonderfully so." He settled his free hand on her lower back beneath the blankets. His palm heated her body, coursing through the thin fabric of the peignoir she wore. It reminded her of how little clothing was between them now. She moved to lie more fully on top of him, spreading her legs a little so she could press her heated core against his hips. He continued to lie still beneath her, his arm lazily propped behind his head as he studied her.

She placed a kiss to his chest, loving the feel of his warm skin beneath her lips as she kissed a path up to his mouth.

"What I wouldn't give to have you beneath me," he whispered between her kisses. His hand on her lower back slid down to her bottom, cupping it in a way that made her flood with wet heat.

She nuzzled his nose and stole a playful kiss. "Why don't you?"

"Because I am *trying* to be a gentleman. Something you're making very difficult, Miss Egerton." He caressed her formal name with a heavy layer of sensuality. His eyes in this light were a dark green that made her think of an English forest in the middle of summer.

She suddenly laughed, which made him laugh too.

"What?" he asked, both of his hands now settling on her bottom beneath the sheets.

"I was thinking of how things would be back in New York if we were courting there."

"Oh?" He stroked his fingers in playful patterns on her backside, toying with the thin material of the night-gown between her flesh and his hands.

"Yes, everyone in New York is so stodgy, the society rules so rigid."

"Worse than here?"

She heard a hint of amusement in his question. "Yes."

Oliver chuckled. "I find that hard to believe. Isn't America built upon the ideas of independence and free spirits?"

"Oh, it is," she insisted. "But there's a rather strong puritanical streak, at least in the northeast, that tends to control modes of behavior. Most of society is run by ladies like the infamous Mrs. Astor, one of the richest and most influential women in America. They belong to what my father says is called the Knickerbocker Club. It's all old-money families that's left them feeling in charge of everything and everyone. They dictate who may attend the balls every year and when social calls must be paid. Ladies have no higher aspirations than to seek a wealthy husband and own a brownstone in Washington Square or Gramercy Park and fill it with an acceptable amount of children. If they could see me now..."

"Mrs. Astor would die of a heart attack," Oliver finished with a wolfish smile. "I've heard my mother talk about her. Even New York society reaches our English ears. I heard she tries to control who can attend what balls."

"She certainly does. But there's always new money coming into New York, and she can't control the waves of the nouveau riche." Rayne grew serious again as she looked down at her tempting English gentleman. "Oliver... Are we moving too fast? I swear I am not a lady of easy virtue, but you make me a little wild."

He cupped her face with one hand. "I know you're not, love. Whatever this is between us, it's overpowering to us both. I won't claim to be a saint, but with you, I've tried to be."

"You don't have to," she said. "I want you to be yourself."

He moved his hand to her throat, curling his fingers around the back of her neck to draw her head down to his. "Even if that means I'm *very* wicked?"

"Yes, be wicked so I won't feel like I'm a temptress," she murmured against his lips before they shared a long, impossibly intimate kiss.

"Very well, my love. I warned you." And it was indeed the only warning she had before he rolled her body beneath his. He shoved the blankets off them, and he kissed his way down to her breasts. She still wore the thin peignoir, and he sucked one hardened nipple through the cloth. The feel of the wet satin and his hungry lips was erotic beyond anything she'd experienced in her girlish fantasies. His hand cupped and kneaded her other breast gently, pinching and rolling the nipple between his thumb and forefinger. Her breasts felt heavy, and her body burned with heat all over as he continued to play with her. Then he moved down her body even farther until he was kneeling between her parted legs, and he pushed her nightgown up.

Rayne tensed, both excited and frightened at being so exposed to him.

"Easy, love," he soothed. "I just want to taste you." He stroked her inner thighs. "Close your eyes. Concentrate on the touch of my hands and my mouth."

He kissed down the inside of her left thigh until he reached her now soaked center. She almost yelped in surprise as he flicked his tongue against the sensitive folds. She lost herself in the strokes of his fingers and the licking of his tongue. It felt as though he wanted to consume her, *all* of her. He explored her, teased and conquered her until she was begging in frantic pants for something she needed more than her own breath. A bold swipe of his tongue was joined by the insertion of two fingers into her tight channel. He stretched her, making it burn enough that she gasped.

Then he thrust those fingers inside her, his pace quickened, and she kept her eyes closed, feeling wild and free in a way she never had before. Then he licked the bud of her arousal, and she exploded with pleasure.

Unable to stop, she reached for him, her hands finding his head, and she fisted her fingers in the silky strands of his dark hair. He continued to lick her and penetrate her with his fingers, drawing out a second, softer climax that stole a breathy moan of exhausted delight from her.

"Wicked..." was all she could whisper.

Oliver's chuckle was accompanied by more kisses as he slid back up her body and claimed her lips. He gave her lower lip a hungry nibble before he kissed her open-mouthed, the kiss raw and primal. It felt wicked too, as though no one should kiss like this, but it was the best sort of kiss. He made her feel beautiful, desired. Their mouths met again and again in a wet, coaxing way that blurred their pleasure into an endless loop for hours. But the sensation of the train coming to a stop dragged both her and Oliver from the sweet aftermath of their passion.

"Have we stopped?" Rayne's head was still fuzzy with desire as she tried to sit up.

"Hold on." Oliver rose and pulled on his dressing gown. He stepped out into the hallway, then returned with a frown.

"What is it?"

"We've stopped at Edinburgh's Waverley Station on Princes Street."

She sat up, pulling her nightgown back down over her knees. "Is that where we should be?"

"Yes, but I saw the conductor on the platform, discussing something with the stationmaster. Why don't you get dressed? I'll do the same, and we'll see what's happened."

Unease prickled at Rayne's insides. "You think something happened?"

"I do, but I'm not sure what."

She rose from the bed and put her dressing gown back on and pulled her cabin key from her pocket. She tucked her feet into her slippers and headed for the door, but Oliver caught her by the waist, pulling her to him for one more scorching kiss.

"Thank you for letting me taste you." He brushed his nose against hers before he pressed his forehead to hers and held her a moment longer before he let her go. Feeling so very vulnerable, she held him back. She hoped he would not think her a clinging sort of woman, but she had never given herself like that to a man, and it felt special for her.

I hope he feels the same.

Then she hurried back to her cabin. She stepped inside to brush her teeth and wash her face. A minute later, Ellen knocked on her door.

"Miss Egerton?"

"Come in, Ellen," she called out.

Her lady's maid entered and began to lay out a dress for the day. "Did you have a nice evening last night?" Ellen inquired.

"I did." She tried not to think about what she and Oliver had done, lest she give herself away with a blush. "And you?"

"Oh yes." Ellen grinned. "I caught up on my reading."

Ellen helped her into a day gown of violet satin. The bodice, sleeves, and white satin underskirt were embroidered with palmetto motifs resembling peacock feathers, made entirely of silver thread. The sleeves were long and the neckline square and low, which would keep her neither too cold nor too hot. Ellen placed a small gold locket around her neck, one that had belonged to Rayne's mother.

Once dressed, she and Ellen stepped into the corridor. She could make out Oliver's form alongside her father's through the windows. Both men were talking to the stationmaster.

"He is handsome, isn't he?" Ellen said beside her.

"Who?"

"Lord Conway." Ellen chuckled.

"He is rather magnificent, isn't he?" She pressed her palm to the glass of the window, drinking in the sight of him. He wore dark-brown trousers and his navy woolen coat lined with fur as he listened to the stationmaster. He had left his top hat back on the train and casually ran a hand through his hair. She flushed as she remem-

bered how it had felt to cling to his hair while his mouth created such divine pleasure inside her.

"Is it true that he means to court you?"

"Yes, how did you know?" She looked at her maid, a little startled.

"Your father mentioned it to me."

"Oh." She relaxed. "Yes, I've agreed." She paused, her eyes still on Oliver. "Do you think it very silly of me? To be so eager for him that I can't seem to think of anything else?"

Ellen grinned at her. "Not at all. So long as the gentleman is treating you well and is worthy of you. Is he?"

"I believe Lord Conway is. When I'm with him, I feel extraordinary, as though anything is possible."

"You do sound smitten by him. But if I might be so bold, sometimes it's easy to let emotions carry us farther than we intend. Could that be the case now? Or do you believe you're falling in love?"

Rayne bit her bottom lip. "I don't believe in love at first sight, nor do I believe I could love a man so soon, but there's something there..." She thought of when he had spoken of his home and his family and how he had seemed so supportive of her need for independence. It was hard not to love a man like that.

"Well, as long as you don't lose your head, I'd say you owe it to yourself to discover the nature of your feelings for him. Just be careful, miss."

Oliver and her father shook hands with the stationmaster before returning to the train. Oliver climbed back inside first.

"It seems the tracks on the way to Inverness are covered in snow. The railway workers are digging them out now, but it will take another day. We will be staying in Edinburgh tonight."

"Oh dear. Will we be able to travel tomorrow morning?" Rayne inquired.

"Yes, if all goes well." Oliver glanced at her father. "I've spoken to Mr. Egerton, and we've both decided it's less comfortable to stay on the train tonight. I've recommended a hotel to him at the base of Edinburgh Castle. We are having our luggage transported there now, and the four of us will take a coach to the hotel."

"I'll pack your valise, Miss Egerton," Ellen said and slipped back into Rayne's cabin.

"Go on ahead with Lord Conway, Rayne. I'll meet you outside with Ellen shortly." Her father returned to his cabin, leaving her and Oliver alone.

She tucked her arm in his as they stepped out onto the platform. Pale winter sunlight came in through the ornate glass dome of Waverley Station and illuminated the booking hall in different splashes of color. Rayne marveled at the unique design. It was prettier than any of the stations they'd seen so far.

"Where are we to stay?" she asked Oliver as they exited the station to hail a hackney.

"A place called the Witchery by the Castle."

"The Witchery?" The name conjured up vivid images of women bent over smoking cauldrons.

"It was built a stone's throw from the spot where convicted witches were burned to death on Castle Hill. The hotel is located in what's now called Boswell Court.

"Did witches used to live nearby? Or were they merely held prisoner at the Witchery?"

"Heavens no." Oliver burst out laughing, and Rayne was torn between laughing with him and jabbing him in the ribs with an elbow.

"The Witchery was formerly a merchant's home in 1595. Then it became a committee chamber for members of the Church of Scotland, then later a rectory. They stopped burning witches around 1720, and the hotel was built as a reminder of the innocent lives lost. I suggested it to your father because it has wonderful cuisine and a broody Jacobean atmosphere, which is not to be missed when you are here in Scotland."

"Jacobean?" The term sounded familiar.

"The Jacobites were Scottish rebels who resisted English rule. You'll see lovely tapestries full of Scottish history hanging there."

Her father and Ellen soon joined them, and Oliver waved down a coach. Rayne claimed a seat where she could pull back the coach curtains and look at the old town of Edinburgh. The city was beautiful, with old sandstone buildings and small narrow passageways between them, which Oliver explained were called closes.

"How do you know so much about Scotland?"

"My great-grandfather and his friends visited here quite often. I have relatives in southern Scotland at Castle Kincaid, and I spent many a Christmas journeying north from Yorkshire."

Rayne leaned against his arm. "That sounds charming."

He grinned, the boyish expression so different from the seductive Oliver she had lain with in his bed that morning, but she adored both versions of him.

"It was. My cousins would build snow forts, and we'd battle for hours until we collapsed in the snow, utterly exhausted."

Rayne's heart stung with envy. "I admit, I'm jealous of you. I have no siblings. I do have cousins, Lord help me." She smiled as she thought of the trouble Uncle Gerard's boys would get into.

"Not fun cousins, I take it?"

"They are, but they are older and all boys. I was left out of most things, including snowball fights."

"What a disappointment. We would have let you play no matter what." His eyes glittered with mischief.

"It is a pity we are too old for snowball fights now."

"Poppycock. You're never too old. How's this for a promise? A battle at Lord Fraser's?"

"Oh, could we?" She almost forgot that the two of them weren't alone in the carriage. She glanced across the seats to see her father and Ellen both watching them, her father with an unreadable expression and Ellen with one of slight worry.

Her father cleared his throat, and Rayne let go of Oliver's arm and scooted a few inches away from him. Her father grunted in approval.

"Well, Lord Conway, since you are so familiar with Edinburgh, what's there to do while we spend the day here?" Her father's gaze was steady on them both. Rayne tried not to think about how closely he was watching them.

"I suggest we take a tour of the castle on the hill. We'll be close to it when we reach the Witchery."

"A castle, eh?" Her father stroked his mustache. "I suppose we haven't toured *too* many of those yet."

"Father, you like all the English and Scottish history," Rayne reminded him. "You read a four-volume set of British history before we left."

Douglas's eyes twinkled. "So I did, so I did. Very well, Miss Moore, could we prevail upon you to join us for a castle tour?"

Ellen blushed and looked toward Rayne. "If you'd like."

"We would love it if you would join us," Rayne assured her.

From the moment they had hired Ellen, Rayne had insisted on making her more of a paid companion than a maid. Ellen had resisted at first, but Rayne had convinced her to embrace a more active role while she worked for them. This meant she had dined with them and attended operas and ballets. Only at certain social functions like balls could they not quite manage to get around the social barriers and allow Ellen to join them.

When the coach stopped on the cobblestone lane of Castle Hill, Oliver leapt out of the coach and was ready to catch Rayne by the waist to help her down. She held her breath as he pulled her close to whisper, "I swear you choose clothing to drive me mad." His gaze swept down the length of her body, focusing for a long moment on the low square neckline.

"You don't like it?" she asked, fishing for a compliment.

"You know I do." He winked as he set her down on the pavement out of the way of the muddy, snow-covered street. Then he assisted Miss Moore down, and Douglas followed behind.

They entered the hotel, where a smartly dressed set of young men greeted them before proceeding outside to collect their luggage from the coach. Oliver and Douglas went to the front desk and collected their room keys.

"Should we all meet down here in half an hour?" Douglas suggested.

Everyone agreed, and they all climbed the stairs to their rooms. Rayne was at the end of the hall, and Oliver's room was beside hers. Their eyes met as they inserted their ornate brass keys into the locks on their doors and turned them at the same time. Oliver's lips curved in a slow, sweet, but also sensual smile before he disappeared into his room.

When she entered hers, she gasped. The room was nothing short of palatial. Red damask wallpaper and dark mahogany wood furniture made the room instantly seem warm and seductive.

Oil lamps by the bed and the fire in the hearth only made the accommodations even more cozy. The tall four-poster bed had gold brocade curtains pulled back against the posts, secured by gold corded ropes with long tassels. A red velvet coverlet draped down over the large bed. Rayne's body heated at the thought of her and Oliver sharing this bed together.

Was she bold enough to invite him here tonight? Yes, she was. Rayne smiled, feeling a little silly as she faced the fact that she was hopeless when it came to Oliver. He made her wild, irresponsible, and desperate for things that an unmarried lady should have no idea existed.

But what did it matter? They were courting now, and if she was honest, she wanted him to propose—the sooner the better. What she felt for him now wasn't simply lust. There were softer, deeper, purer emotions in her heart now. She was afraid to call it love just yet, but perhaps it was. Ellen was right that she should discover what her true feelings were for Oliver.

Her mother and father had fallen in love right away and married within a month. Neither of them had ever doubted each other or their quick marriage. It gave

Rayne hope that she and Oliver might share the same good fortune.

She removed her hat and gloves and sat down on the edge of the bed. She took in the surroundings of the chamber. A portion of the wall suddenly began to shift and move, and she almost shrieked. Then the sight of Oliver's face peering around the edge of the door had her giggling.

She grabbed the nearest pillow and threw it at his head. "You frightened me!"

He pulled the door closed enough to shield himself from the projectile, and when he seemed certain she wouldn't throw another, he stepped into the room.

"Did you know the door was there?" she asked as he closed the door behind him. She could barely see the line in the wall, it had sealed so seamlessly.

"I *may* have been aware of it when your father and I requested rooms," he admitted with a devilish chuckle. Then he stalked toward her, and she gave a shriek of laughter as he tried to pounce on her on the bed. She rolled onto her hands and knees and crawled away from him.

"How the devil can you move so fast in so much clothing?" he demanded as he circled around the bed and caught her by the waist, pulling her into his arms.

"Practice." She grinned at him as he swooped down and kissed her senseless. Then he simply held her in his arms, and his lips brushed the crown of her hair.

"Perhaps we can skip the castle tour," he murmured.

"As much as I would love to, my father would be sure to notice our absence."

Oliver chuckled. "That means I must marry you sooner rather than later so I can take you to bed anytime we wish without the fear of drawing parental wrath."

She looked up at him, hope surging in her. But what if he was only teasing?

"Oliver...," she began, not that she had the faintest idea what she wanted to say.

"Too soon, I suppose?" He smiled ruefully. "You deserve a lavish proposal on the top of some majestic mountain, or in the midst of a glittering ballroom—"

"Oliver," she said, interrupting him, "please don't tease me about such things, not when I..."

He cupped her chin. "When you what?"

She looked away, wanting desperately to hide her embarrassment.

"Tell me, love."

She burrowed closer to him, wondering if he would pull away if she told him the truth.

"When I wish for it." She paused. "That, and truth. A lady ought not to tell a man that, but I feel that way, and I want only honesty between us. We've only known each other for two days, and yet I feel a bit in love with you already. I hope it leads to more." *So much more,* she thought.

Oliver was silent a long moment, and when she finally turned her face to his, his eyes were soft and a green color that reminded her of freshly cut grass on the lawns of a beautiful estate. He made her think of summer garden parties where the ladies wore white frothy lace-trimmed gowns, and Rayne would play a bit of tennis with her cousins and bask in the glow of the sun.

"I wasn't teasing, Rayne," he said. "From the moment we met, I have wanted you, *all* of you. I have marriage in mind, and as long as you like me, I shall continue to woo you to that end, my love."

"To marriage? What if you decide I'm too tiresome or boring or—"

He silenced her with another kiss that left her feeling scorched in the best way.

"Somehow, I don't believe that's possible." He played with a lock of her hair that fell over her shoulder. She was all too aware that they were standing chest to chest, with her trapped against the tall bed.

"You tempt me, my love. Tempt me so much," he warned, then stepped back. "But unfortunately, your father will come searching for us if we don't meet him downstairs."

"I need a moment. I shall meet you in the corridor."

Oliver stole a final feathery kiss and left her alone.

Rayne pressed her hands to her flushed face and smiled...smiled like a fool in love.

9

Oliver delighted in showing Rayne around Edinburgh Castle. A heavy fog rolled across the snow-covered grounds, and he had been lucky enough to steal her away into an alcove, unseen by her father and Miss Moore, for a quick, passionate kiss on more than one occasion. It had become a game for them, to see how many times he could corner his little American before they had to reappear and act as if nothing scandalous had happened.

He couldn't keep his hands off her. She was addictive. Her smile, her laughter, the way she focused so intently on learning the history of this place—it all fascinated him. He had spoken the truth at the Witchery, and while her fortune had allowed for the possibility of pursuing her, that fortune held no sway over how he felt. If he were the one with the fortune and she were penniless, he would have chosen her to be his wife without a second thought. He didn't want to think about what his life would have been like if he'd never met her at Lady Poole's ball. He was a slave to his circumstances, but good fortune had given him Rayne as a possible match, and he wanted her desperately.

His family would adore her. Zadie had already gotten along famously with her, and his mother would admire Rayne's intelligence and sweetness. Everett would appreciate her wit and playfulness. And Oliver? He loved all of her.

I'm a blessed man.

He followed her and Ellen now into a clothing store on the Royal Mile, where ready-made items were sold. The two ladies gathered around a rack of woolen tartan scarves in an array of colorful plaids.

"Oliver, come try on a scarf. You would look so dashing." Rayne plucked a scarf from the shelves as she glanced his way.

He reluctantly joined them. He could not buy anything. He'd spent too much already on his hotel room, but he had needed to impress Rayne and her father. If they suspected he was as destitute as he was, he could lose Rayne forever. And he couldn't bear that, because like her, he was falling in love. There was no other way to describe it. Whenever he was near her, it was like he was falling into orbit around a bright and beautiful star.

Yet I deceive her with every breath. The dark thought encroached on his happiness.

Rayne wrapped a red-and-green plaid scarf around his neck and eyed it critically.

"Ellen, don't you think this brings out his eyes?"

"It certainly does, Miss Egerton," Ellen replied, but she cast a worried glance at Oliver. He attempted to remove the scarf, but Rayne tutted and kept it around his neck.

"I shall get it for you," she said.

"Rayne, you mustn't—" he protested.

"For Christmas," she replied in a tone that brooked no argument.

"Rayne, *no*. I don't need gifts." He caught her wrist, hating the look of hurt he saw in her eyes. But what else could he do? When she found out about his financial circumstances, he did not want her looking back on this moment and seeing it as him using her. He was not after her fortune for himself. His family and his home needed it, but not him. He could continue to wear old clothes and not renew his club membership and even keep sharing his valet with his brother if it meant keeping Rayne in his life.

Rayne folded the scarf back up and set it down on the counter. She turned sharply away from him. This was going badly. He started to reach for her, but his hand dropped back to his side. What could he say to correct his foolishness? He looked at Ellen, and she was frowning at him, not in disapproval, but disappointment.

"I only meant... I don't want you to think..." But he

found no way to finish his thought in a way that worked. Oliver left the shop and stood out in the cold next to Douglas, who was admiring the streets of Edinburgh.

"Everything all right?" Douglas asked.

"Yes, of course. I simply had to excuse myself before Rayne purchased half the shop for me. I think she wants to see me in a kilt." Oliver was not about to admit that he had upset Rayne.

Douglas laughed. "That does sound like Rayne, always a bit romantic."

"There's nothing wrong with that. It's simply too bloody cold for a man to wear a kilt with all this snow." Oliver watched Rayne and Ellen move through the shop from his vantage point on the street where he and Douglas could peer through the shop windows.

When the ladies emerged from the shop, the smile on Rayne's face seemed off somehow. They spent the rest of the day touring museums and galleries close to the Royal Mile, which led from the castle down the sloping hill. Rayne seemed to be in better spirits by the time they had dinner. Douglas was a man of taste, and he told Oliver he wished to try the cuisine in Scotland, which meant they feasted upon tasty meat pies and drank whiskey at a small and cozy restaurant. It was located across from Greyfriars Kirkyard—a cemetery—which wasn't nearly as macabre as one might think. It was a relief to see Rayne's natural smile return as he explained the history of Edinburgh to everyone over dinner.

As evening fell, he could see Rayne and Ellen were growing weary from walking. He couldn't imagine them carrying their skirts all day to keep them out of the snowy puddles on the streets and pavement without becoming exhausted.

"Shall we turn in for the evening, since we'll need to be ready at the station tomorrow morning?" Douglas posed as the four of them entered the hotel lobby.

"Yes," Rayne sighed. "My feet ache something fierce, Father. All I want is to crawl into bed and sleep." Her nose wrinkled as she removed her gloves and her red velvet dolman. Oliver wanted to sweep her up in his arms and carry her to the nearest claw-foot bathtub, strip her naked, and join her for a hot bath. But he knew she was still upset, and he needed to explain, at least enough to tell her why she couldn't spend any money on him.

He returned to his own room and removed his gloves and coat before opening the connecting door between their rooms. He found her sitting alone at the rosewood vanity table, gazing at herself in the mirror with a lost expression on her face. Tears coated her cheeks, and her wet skin shimmered in the candlelight.

"Rayne, my love." She tensed at his words, and her eyes looked to his in the reflection. She brushed the tears away and faced him, that same false cheeriness cutting him deep.

"I'm sorry, I was woolgathering." She focused on smoothing her gown, no longer looking at him. Oliver came over and knelt at her feet and clasped her hands in his, stilling that frantic nervous fluttering of her fingers over the satin.

"I want to apologize for today. But I cannot let you buy me things."

"Why not? Is it some silly English custom I don't know about?" She tried to sound as if she didn't care, but she couldn't hide the hurt in her tone.

"No." He drew a fortifying breath. "My family is not as wealthy as yours. We live more frugally, and I don't want you to ever think I want you to have to buy things for me. I already hate that I cannot do so for you, as much as I would like to."

"Oliver..." She pulled her hands free of his and cupped his face. "I'm sorry, I didn't know," she said, and much to his surprise, she leaned in to kiss him. It was not quite the reaction he'd expected.

"I was too embarrassed to tell you. You mean so much to me, and I was afraid you would think less of me because I can't buy you lavish gifts in kind."

She slid off the chair and fell to her knees in front of him. "I don't need lavish gifts. I only need you."

He placed his hands on her cheeks the same way she was with him. "I hope that never changes."

"It won't," she vowed.

Lord, he wanted to believe that. But it was one thing

to admit he was not wealthy—quite another to admit he was destitute.

"Oliver, stay with me tonight." She stood and pulled him close. The woman was such a tempting bundle of sweetness and satin.

"If that is what you wish." He captured her lips with his, wanting to growl in heady desire at the way she melted in his arms.

"I do, and I want *more*."

He slid his hands down her back. "More?"

"So much more." She looked at him with those soft bedroom eyes. "I want everything."

"Then let me give it to you."

OLIVER KISSED HER DEEPLY, A SENSUAL PROMISE lingering between them. Rayne shivered. She wanted him, *needed* him tonight. And he'd promised to be with her. Her head swam a little, and she giggled. It felt like the first time she'd taken one of her father's bottles of sherry as a sixteen-year-old and sampled a bit too much of it.

Oliver began to unfasten the hooks at the back of her gown as they continued to kiss. When her gown loosened, she shimmied out of it and slipped off the bed to stand in front of him. Then, with a nervous beat of her heart, she turned her back to him so he could unlace her corset. The second he began to pull the laces loose, she felt like she could breathe for the first time in ages. The whalebone corset dropped to the ground, and she turned to face him just as he began to lift the thin chemise she wore off her body.

She stood bare before him now, except for her stockings and boots. His gaze raked down her body, and she felt a flood of heat deep in her belly. He pulled her against him, her bare breasts brushing against his satin waistcoat.

"There's nothing more arousing than holding a beautiful naked woman in my arms." He kissed the shell of her ear in a way that made her quiver. Then he sank to one knee and began rolling down her stockings and unlacing her boots. By the time she was completely naked before him, he had soothed her trembling nerves with kisses and caresses. He was a master of this. He knew exactly what to do with women.

"Oliver, how many others have you been with?" This was more a matter of curiosity than jealousy. There was no way he could be this well versed in seduction without practice.

Oliver cupped her chin, and his free hand settled on her lower back. "There have been a few, but you are the one I feel I've been waiting my whole life for." His lips seared a path from her neck to her shoulders, and his words wrapped her heart in soft velvet. She stood on her tiptoes to kiss him back, and then she pulled at the buttons of his waistcoat. He let her undress him, let her explore his body, and all the while he caressed her, touched her, and left burning kisses on her skin.

Rayne had never touched a man like this before. She coasted her palms up his chest and bent her head to flick her tongue against his nipple. She smiled in delight at the way he groaned and held her close in encouragement.

"I'm going to make love to you tonight," he vowed as he unfastened his trousers and let them fall to the floor.

"You'd better." Rayne reached for him, sliding one hand from his corded abs to his hard length. She stroked him hard as he bent his head to hers for a kiss. Then he curled his fingers around her wrist and gently removed her hand from his shaft.

"But if you touch me like that, my love, I fear I won't last."

"Oh..." She blushed and then squeaked in surprise as he scooped her up and set her on the bed. She fell onto her back as he climbed up the length of her body and caged her beneath him.

She parted her legs, though it was a little nerve-racking to let his large body settle between them. Despite his size compared to hers, he didn't crush her as he lay down on top of her.

"Touch me now, however you wish," Oliver said. He bent his head to her neck and kissed a spot that made her writhe under him.

"Oh, Oliver..." She arched her back and pressed

close. His cock nudged her entrance, but she was still too nervous to let him inside.

He didn't rush her. He simply kissed her, and soon she was relaxing into his tender seduction. Before she could even think about it, she canted her hips up at the same time he guided himself to her and thrust inside. It felt natural, good, and then she whimpered at the pinching pain deep inside her.

Oliver's mouth continued to work its midnight magic on her, and the pain faded into memory. His soft breath fanned her face as he withdrew, leaving behind an ancient ache for more. Then he thrust back inside, and they shared a moment of deepest pleasure. She never wanted his body to leave hers. Their connection felt almost mystical. Her inner walls tightened around him as he surged in and out, slow at first and then faster until she could barely catch her breath and her heart was galloping away. Oliver continued to imprison her beneath him as he claimed her. She welcomed it, clung to him, and basked in the wild passion, knowing that he belonged to her in this moment too.

"Oliver, I...love you." She spoke the words and couldn't take them back. His eyes widened, and he sank into her again. Stars burst before her eyes. Oliver cursed and breathed her name, his body rigid as he emptied himself inside her. She relaxed beneath him, sated in a way that defied all reason. When he next spoke, his words stunned her.

"Marry me, Rayne."

Her fingers dug slightly into his shoulders as she held on to him. "You mean it?"

"You love me, and I feel the same way. Why should we wait?" His eyes were still dark with passion, but she heard the sincerity in his voice.

"Then yes!" Joy fluttered inside her, and she kissed him. A kiss that spoke of the excitement and tender longing that had welled up within her.

"You've made me the happiest man." He kissed the tip of her nose. "Stay here a minute."

He moved off her body, and she missed his warmth right away. He stepped into her bathing chamber, and she heard the sound of bath taps turning on. Then he returned and scooped her up, carrying her into the bathing room, where he set her down beside the massive claw-foot tub. He tested the water, and when it was warm enough, he climbed in and motioned for her to join him. She winced a little as her lower body was still sore from their lovemaking, and he cradled her against his chest as the warm water spilled over them. Rayne closed her eyes and surrendered to the feeling of pure bliss.

"I didn't hurt you, did I?" Oliver asked. "I've never been with a virgin before."

"It hurt but a moment, and then you made it feel wonderful." She lifted one of his hands to her lips and kissed his long elegant fingers.

"I meant it, Rayne—I want you to marry me. But I don't want you to answer when you're overwhelmed with passion. Just think on it." He stroked a hand down her belly and caressed her mound beneath the water. Rayne whimpered as he slid one finger into her still sore channel.

"Yes. I want you, Oliver." Yes, she was overwhelmed by passion, but she knew her own mind and her heart.

"Tell me again in the morning. I won't be upset if you need time."

"Oliver, we've known each other but a handful of days, yet it feels like I've loved you my entire life. I won't need time."

"I feel the same." He kissed her cheek and wrapped his arms around her. She couldn't help but think every-thing was perfect. She was going to have a marriage like her parents, one full of love.

OLIVER CARRIED RAYNE BACK TO BED. SHE HAD fallen asleep in the tub with him. Now she lay naked in his arms in her bed, and he brushed the backs of his fingers over her cheek, watching her sleep before he turned the oil lamps down to low.

But he couldn't find sleep. It eluded him as worries built in the back of his mind. He would have to talk with Douglas tomorrow and get his blessing. And he would have to find a way to make sure that Rayne approved of her dowry being used at once for his family and his home. The whole thought of it gave him a headache. He didn't want to think or worry about money with Rayne. He wanted to marry her, declare his affection, and carry her off to Astley Court, where he could give her a home and a family.

But what if it all went wrong? What if, when she learned the truth, she thought him a heartless fortune hunter? This and other thoughts haunted him well past when the fire died and dawn was on the horizon.

10

Rayne fell in love with the Scottish Highlands as she descended from the train that afternoon and stepped into the city of Inverness. The train ride from Edinburgh to Inverness had taken five hours, but she'd enjoyed every minute of it. The countryside was defined by high peaks, heathery moors, and serene lakes—or lochs, as the locals called them—which spread across the landscape. Snow covered half the fields and topped the tall hills. The train had carried them through towns that had such delightful names as Boat of Garten and Feshiebridge. Oliver had told her that this far north in Scotland a mass of small villages were all tucked into a wilderness of pine and heather where bitter winters and hot summers divided the year.

Rayne now stood on High Street in Inverness, a cold wind teasing her heavy red velvet skirts as she took in the town. Oliver joined her as she studied the looming edifice of Inverness Castle. It was a bulky work of stone. A statue of a beautiful young woman stood at the front of the esplanade. The woman's face seemed anxious as she looked toward the southwest.

"What is she looking toward?" Rayne asked, drawing closer to it.

"The Isle of Skye. That is Flora MacDonald."

"Who's that?"

Oliver put an arm around her waist. "A very brave woman. She helped Bonnie Prince Charlie flee Culloden's battlefield and sail to the Isle of Skye."

Rayne stared at the stone woman, wondering how she must have felt as she helped the man who had almost ruled Scotland, but instead had fled for his life. "What happened to her?"

"She was arrested after Charles escaped. She was a sympathetic cause for many in England and was eventually released from the Tower of London. She married a captain in the British Army and lived on the Isle of Skye for a time."

Rayne looked once more at the baronial turrets of Inverness Castle and its pink sandstone walls. "Are we very far from Culloden?"

"Not far at all, actually," Oliver said. "It's an old moor, a quiet place. I visited there as a boy with my father. I swear I could feel the spirits of the clanspeople who had fallen that day. Their anguished cries seemed to drift up from the haunting grounds, making it hard to breathe. I was not proud to be English that day, I can tell you. To see the lonely place where the way of life in the Highlands was lost forever is enough to break any man's heart." He paused in quiet contemplation before continuing. "Though I do like coming here when I can. The Highlands have a quiet and natural peace. It reminds me of Yorkshire."

Rayne curled her arm in his as they turned away and headed for the waiting coach. Her father waved to them as they crossed the bustling street and joined them at the coach.

The ride to Lord Fraser's didn't take very long, and yet their imminent arrival brought out a fresh excitement for Rayne. Oliver had told her he planned to ask for her father's blessing once they were settled in.

Lord Fraser's manor house was nestled within an old forest. To Rayne, it seemed like a place one would find a slumbering wood god lurking within the heart of one of its massive trees. Perhaps it was a fanciful idea, but she rather liked the magical feel of these Scottish forests.

Lord Fraser's house was a lovely Georgian-era mansion that seemed to have been molded out of a medieval castle. When the coach stopped, a footman wearing the Earl of Fraser's livery came out to meet them. Rayne and Ellen were shown to their chambers, and Rayne changed out of her damp traveling clothes and into a pleasant day gown of blue faille brocade trimmed with aged cream lace. It was a more delicate gown, one best suited to being worn indoors. The blue and gold of the faille brocade made her feel warm, as though summer was upon her. As she left her bedchamber, she met a tall handsome man in his early forties in the corridor.

"Miss Egerton?" he asked, his Scottish accent rolling off his tongue.

"Yes?"

"I am Lord Fraser. I'm sorry I was not able to greet you and your father when you arrived. I was seeing to some business." He bowed over her hand and lightly kissed her knuckles. She admired his dark-brown hair, cut a little too long to be fashionable, and the hazel gleam of mischief in his eyes. He was a bachelor, according to all the gossip in London, but well sought after. She'd heard whispers that the woman Fraser had loved had married another, and he'd vowed never to love again. It was a pity that such a charming man wanted nothing more to do with love.

"It's a pleasure to meet you, Lord Fraser. I cannot tell you how honored we are to be here for the holidays."

Lord Fraser smiled and offered his arm. "Let me take you downstairs." He spoke about his home and the rich history of it, such as how his family had helped hide Bonnie Prince Charlie one night. He lifted his chin in pride as he spoke. By the time they reached the morning room, where some of the other guests were spending the afternoon, Rayne was in high spirits.

Until she saw Adelaide Berwick.

The moment Adelaide's eyes locked with hers, all of

Rayne's joy and excitement evaporated. Adelaide's face was pinched with open displeasure as though she, too, was surprised at Rayne's appearance.

Rayne glanced around at the dozen or so guests, and her heart dropped even further. Zadie wasn't here yet, but then she remembered that Oliver had said they would be a few days late. What would she do without a friend to help her lessen the sting of whatever cruel things Adelaide had in store for her? She had handled Adelaide at Lady Poole's ball, but she hadn't liked being harsh to another woman like that. It wasn't in her nature to be mean-spirited, even to someone like Adelaide.

Now more than ever, Rayne wished her mother were alive to counsel her on how to handle this situation. She didn't see her father anywhere and had no idea where he'd gone. She knew no one else in the room except Lord Fraser, who was now conversing with his other guests. Even Oliver was absent. Feeling awkward and alone, Rayne selected a book off the nearest table and took a seat by the window. She didn't read; rather, she watched the reflections of the people in the room like faint specters in the glass.

Adelaide and her mother were talking, their heads bent together as they whispered. Rayne tried not to shift restlessly in her chair, but it was hard to ignore them. They were almost certainly talking about her. When she couldn't take it anymore, she stood and started toward the door, but Adelaide stepped in between her and the exit.

"I heard you arrived here with Lord Conway?" Adelaide's tone was far too sweet to be genuine.

"Yes. We did have the pleasure of his company. Are you acquainted with him?" Rayne was proud of herself for sounding civil. It wasn't easy. Adelaide seemed to bring out the worst in her.

"Acquainted?" Adelaide smiled. "Oh yes, quite so. His estate borders mine. We've been friends since we were children. His father and mine were old friends. We are excited to be uniting our families soon."

It took a moment for Rayne to understand what she meant.

"You are to marry Everett?"

Adelaide laughed, the sound as sharp as broken glass. "Everett? Heavens no. No, *Oliver* and I have been betrothed for years now. I'm old enough now that my father will let me marry. He wished for me to wait until I was twenty."

"You and..." Oliver's name turned to ash upon her tongue. Dread settled inside her chest like a dark cloud smothering all light and life.

"Yes, of course." She shrugged a shoulder as if what she had said was completely obvious. "After all, he needs to marry well, what with his family being in such dire straits."

Dire straits... The words echoed in Rayne's mind.

Oliver had said they were living frugally, but that wasn't the same as dire straits.

Rayne tried to wrap her mind around what Adelaide was saying. Adelaide fixed her with a cunning look, as though sensing she'd found Rayne's weak spot.

"He isn't going to marry for love, only money. And I want him, so my father is more than happy to pay him the dowry he needs." Adelaide played with the lace cuff on her left wrist as she smiled too sweetly at Rayne. "They say his family will lose Astley Court in a month if he doesn't marry soon."

Rayne felt as though Adelaide had pushed her into a freshly dug grave and was now shoveling dirt upon her.

"Oh, I say, you look far too pale. Perhaps you ought to rest until dinner." Adelaide patted Rayne's cheek condescendingly. Rayne slapped her hand away and stumbled back, almost tripping over the train of her gown in her haste to escape this vile woman's poisonous touch.

Rayne fled the morning room, hoping to escape the stares of the other guests. But as she reached the entryway, she froze at the sight of Oliver in the hall greeting Zadie, a man who looked too much like Oliver not to be his brother, and a lovely older woman. His family had arrived early? A few minutes ago she would have been overjoyed, but now it felt as though she were hearing an old grandfather clock ticking away her doom as she would have to face the family of a man she could no longer marry.

"Rayne! Come meet my family." Oliver smiled at her, that warm, inviting smile that she wanted so badly to trust. Now part of her wanted to slap that smile off his face.

Two days—you've only known him two days. How could you be such a fool to fall for a fortune hunter?

Then she realized that love didn't come quickly, only lust. She had very foolishly confused the two and played right into his hands. Oliver wanted her money, not her. He must have discovered that she was a bigger prize than Adelaide.

"Rayne." Oliver came over to her and grasped her hands in his. "Are you all right? You look pale."

"I..." She didn't dare let him know that he had ripped her heart out of her chest.

"Come meet my family."

Everything inside her screamed for her to run away. But she was stuck. Zadie and the others came up to her.

"Rayne! It's so lovely to see you again!" Zadie hugged her, and Rayne returned her embrace, but she felt nothing. Had Zadie been the one to tell Oliver she was rich? Had she been scouring the London balls looking for someone exactly like her? A dozen questions were carried on black wings of despair, but she didn't ask them. She didn't want to know the answers.

"This is my mother, Margaret, and my brother, Everett." Oliver beamed at his family. Rayne wished with all her heart that she could have had this moment in truth, with no lies, no secrets.

"It's wonderful to meet you, Miss Egerton. Oliver was telling us all about you," Margaret said.

"Was he?" she asked faintly.

"Oh yes. He was singing your praises." Everett grinned at her, and Rayne tried to smile, but it was far too late.

"It's lovely to meet you, but I really must go upstairs and rest. I'm feeling rather faint right now."

"Please, let me help you." Oliver moved toward her, but she shrank back from him.

"No, please, see to your family." She rushed up the stairs, leaving him behind. By the time she reached her chambers, her vision had blurred with tears. What was she going to do? She couldn't marry him now—she couldn't. Not when he'd become the thing she'd always feared.

It was all so clear now. Oliver had sought her out on the train. Why else would he have traveled alone while his family came later? And Zadie knew she was rich— far richer than Adelaide. And he'd already sung her praises, according to Everett, yet they had only just arrived. All the dreaded pieces of a wretched puzzle clicked into place. This had all been planned. He'd hunted her with the cleverness of the most talented fortune hunter.

I should leave today. Board the train and return to London with Ellen.

Women traveled alone on trains all the time. She could wait in London for her father to finish his business with Lord Fraser and return. It would be rude to abandon the house party, but she couldn't stay here, not with that man staying here.

Oliver stared up the stairs in the direction of where Rayne had gone, and he didn't like the sudden knot of dread forming inside him. She hadn't been her usual happy self. Not that he didn't expect her, like all people, to have an off moment. But what he'd seen in her face...it had been pain of a different sort. She'd looked at him with an agony he couldn't fathom having caused. What could have happened in the hour he'd left her alone while he'd gotten settled and scheduled a meeting with Lord Fraser?

"Is she all right?" his mother asked. "She looked very pale."

"Yes, I think so," he replied, but the words held the lingering bitter taste of a lie. Something terrible had happened, but he wasn't sure what. His mother watched him with anxious eyes.

"I know you are feeling pressured, but two days is quick, Oliver. You shouldn't rush this, not if you care about her as much as you say you do."

"I love her, Mother. I know it sounds naïve to say it so soon, but I do. I love her in a way I never thought I would love any woman. She is intelligent and passionate and sweet." But it was more than that. Rayne made life seem full of endless excitement. There was a steadiness to her, a feeling that he could spend his life with her and that even the soft, quiet moments would have their own intimate thrill.

"If you love her, then I know we shall as well." His mother embraced him before she looked to Zadie and Everett. "Let's get settled. We shall meet down here before dinner."

Oliver watched them leave and then checked his pocket watch. He was to meet with Lord Fraser shortly, but before then he had to find Rayne's father and ask for his blessing.

"Oliver?" A feminine voice stilled him just as he reached the base of the stairs.

He turned around. "Adelaide." He turned to leave, but she spoke again.

"Oliver... I know."

That knot of dread inside him only grew. "Know what?"

"About your family's unfortunate situation." Adelaide's eyes seemed guileless, but he saw a faint hint of cruel victory hovering around them.

He came toward her, trying to rein in his temper. "And how would you know that?"

"Because my father is friends with Mr. Kelly of Drummonds. He knew that our parents always hoped we would make a match. Well..." She smiled prettily. "I am ready to accept your proposal."

The cold triumph within Adelaide's gaze turned his

stomach. This was why he had avoided her, why he had fled to Lady Poole's library, desperate to avoid this moment, to avoid becoming her pawn.

"Adelaide, I'm sorry. I've already proposed to another, and she has accepted."

The smile slid from Adelaide's face. "It's that American, isn't it? I feared you might have a dalliance with her, but I thought perhaps you had better sense. Breeding is at least as important as money, after all." Adelaide spoke more to herself, but then her gaze focused on him again. "It's a good thing I warned her about you, then. She had no idea that you were fortune hunting. Fortunately, it seems I saved her from that fate."

A wave of panic caused Oliver's blood to pound inside his head. He almost stumbled with the dizziness of it.

"You did *what?*"

"I told her the truth. That you need money. That you need an heiress. You don't need love, but you *do* need full bank accounts." Adelaide smirked. "I believe the foolish little girl thought herself in love with you." Her tone now became accusatory. "How cruel of you to string her along like that. At least I understand how these things work. She's a stranger in these parts, and quite vulnerable to someone like you."

"She is, and I'm in love with her." He wanted to grab Adelaide and shake her.

A flicker of shock flashed on her face at the mention

of his loving Rayne, but it was covered all too quickly. "You can't be. There is no room for love in our world, only obligation. You knew she had more money than my family, so I can hardly blame your choice, but honestly. Love? You can't love a stranger in only two days. Some people can't fall in love even after a lifetime."

"She isn't a stranger to me. Not anymore." He dragged a hand through his hair. "Adelaide, how could you do this to me?"

"How could *I*?" she hissed. "You were supposed to be mine, Oliver. From the moment I was born, my father and yours hoped we would marry. And you just tossed me aside for some American with no pedigree?"

Oliver stared at Adelaide in horror. "Do you wish to know why I wouldn't propose to you? It's because you're selfish and spiteful. Rayne is everything you aren't, and I would marry her even if she had not a shilling to her name."

"You don't fool me!" Adelaide snapped. "You need her money. *That's* what you love."

Oliver shook his head, his mind racing. It wasn't about the money, not anymore. That moment he realized what he said was true. The only thing that mattered to him was Rayne, and he couldn't afford to lose her.

"I don't have time for this. I have to fix the mess you've made." He spun away and raced up to the hall of rooms that had been prepared for the guests. He caught the attention of an upstairs maid whose arms were full of fresh linens.

"Excuse me, which room is Miss Egerton staying in?"

"The last room on the right." The maid gestured behind her.

"Thank you." He raced down to the end of the corridor and knocked on Rayne's door. He waited and heard the sound of a dress whispering on the carpets.

"Who is it?" Rayne's voice was muffled, but he could hear an unfamiliar roughness to her tone. Had she been crying? The thought tore him apart.

"It's me, Oliver," he said.

There was a long silence, and then, "*Please*, go away. I'm not feeling well, and I don't wish to see anyone."

"Rayne, please," he begged softly, resting his forehead against the closed door.

"No." The reply was firm and hit him like a slap to the face.

"Please. I spoke to Adelaide. If you just let me in, I'll explain."

The door swung open so fast he stumbled and clutched the doorjamb. Rayne stood there with tear-stained cheeks and puffy eyes.

"There is nothing to explain. You want to marry me for my money, and I don't want that. Our engagement is off, Lord Conway. You're free to marry your childhood sweetheart. I'm sure her family has enough for your needs."

"My childhood sweetheart?" He stumbled over the words in shock. "Adelaide? We were never... She wasn't..."

"I don't care either way what she is or isn't. I'm just glad I learned the truth before I tied myself to you forever." Rayne slammed the door shut, and he heard the lock slide into place.

Oliver leaned against the door for what felt like forever, his chest tight. He had lost the only woman he had wanted to make a life with.

"Oliver?" Everett's voice made him lift his head.

"Everett," he sighed. "I'm sorry. I'm not in the mood." He couldn't handle his brother's teasing just now, not when his chest felt like it had been cracked open and someone had stolen his heart from between his ribs. He could barely breathe. Everything had been going so well, and now all was lost—Rayne was lost.

"What happened?"

"I've lost her, Everett. Adelaide told her I wanted her for her money." He mumbled this confession against Rayne's closed door, feeling trapped more than he ever had in his life. Trapped because he'd lost the one thing that truly mattered.

Everett crossed his arms. "Don't you?"

"There was necessity to consider, of course, but I *never* only wanted the money. I wanted Rayne too." Oliver stepped away from the door and dropped his hand in defeat. Clinging to her door wouldn't make her change her mind. Nothing could do that.

"Oliver, if you love her, would you be willing to give up Astley Court, give up all we have?"

"I would, but I couldn't do that to you, Mother, and Zadie."

Everett stepped close and put his hands on Oliver's shoulders. "Forget the rest of us and just think. You and Miss Egerton. Would you give it all up for her?"

"Yes," Oliver replied without hesitation. "If she wanted me without a fortune, I'd live in a tiny cottage with one room just to be with her."

"Then do it." Oliver flashed a Cheshire cat grin. "Choose her, not the money. Her father could draw up a legal settlement that transfers most of his money elsewhere and gives her a tiny livable allowance. Then you can go to her and prove to her that it isn't the money you want and that you want to marry her without it."

"But what about you? What about Mother and Zadie?" Oliver stared at Everett, shocked to see his rakish brother putting the needs of others before his own.

"Trust me, we will be fine. We would all prefer to live in poverty rather than have you brokenhearted and forced to marry the dreaded Adelaide Berwick. To be honest, I was not looking forward to spending the holidays with her."

Oliver's heart swelled with love for his younger brother.

"Thank you, Everett." There was so much else he wanted to say, but he couldn't seem to form the words.

"Now go. You've got a man to see about a bride." Everett laughed and gently pushed Oliver toward the stairs. Oliver rushed down to find a footman who could show him where Lord Fraser was. Once he had his future as Fraser's London steward secured, he would seek out Mr. Egerton. He prayed he could have it all fixed by tonight, and he would have Rayne in his arms again where she belonged.

❧ II ❧

Rayne and Ellen had their luggage packed, and a footman was summoned to carry it down to Lord Fraser's coach.

"Are you certain you wish to leave?" Ellen asked as they stood in the entry hall, waiting for their dolmans to be brought to them.

The old Scottish manor house was full of Christmas cheer, with evergreen garlands covering the banister of the stairs and kissing boughs hung over more than one doorway. The wooden floors creaked, and the tapestries whispered with Christmas secrets. Rayne would have given anything to stay here, to embrace the magic of the holidays in a home like this, but she couldn't face Oliver again.

"Ellen, I can't stay," she whispered. "Everything I believed about Lord Conway was a lie."

She had confessed to her maid what had transpired

between her and Oliver. Not everything, but enough that Ellen knew Oliver had secretly been a fortune hunter all along like all the other men who had wished to court her in the past and failed to win her hand. But this time, she had fallen hard. She'd been so careful before to never let a man play upon her affections in order to get at her money, but somehow Oliver had done it flawlessly.

Ellen was quiet as they put on their dolmans and walked down to the coach. Rayne had written her father a letter, as well as one for Lord Fraser, apologizing for her abrupt departure. She left them in her room for the house maid to deliver when she came to tidy up. Rayne knew that leaving would cause the ladies to gossip, but she wouldn't be there to care. She would return to London and wait for her father to join her. Then they would return home to New York. Life would go on as before, somehow.

They arrived at the train station ahead of schedule. For a while neither of them spoke, leaving Rayne to ruminate on her heartbreak and Ellen to look on uncomfortably. Finally, Ellen spoke and broke Rayne's painful thoughts.

"Miss Egerton, I feel I must tell you something. I hope I will not lose my position over it, but I believe it's important." Ellen touched Rayne's hand gently.

Something had clearly been vexing Ellen for the entire carriage ride, but Rayne had assumed it was concern for her. "What is it?"

A frown creased Ellen's brow. "Before you employed me, I worked as a lady's maid for Lord Conway's sister."

"Zadie?" Rayne gasped.

"Yes." Ellen went pale with anxiety.

"You knew Lord Conway this entire time? Why didn't you tell me?" Rayne stared at her maid, wondering if Ellen had been working with Oliver somehow, helping to bring them together or to deceive her.

"Lord Conway asked me not to when he discovered I was on the train and I was working for you. I warned you to be cautious, not because he isn't a good man—he is—but I wanted you both to fall in love. I thought I owed it to him to keep his secret for a time until he could tell you himself."

"Another lie," Rayne muttered and closed her eyes. She felt so cut open, so hurt that her heart felt raw. Even Ellen, a woman she had grown to consider a friend, had played a part in this awful deception.

"No, you don't understand," Ellen insisted.

"What's there to understand? He's brought everyone around him in on his scheme to marry me for my inheritance."

"I simply wish you to understand, miss. Lord Conway's father died a year and a half ago. He hid his bad investments from his family, and it came as a harsh blow. The Conways were not one for extravagance before, but after, when Lord Conway—Oliver, I mean—began to unravel the mess his father had left behind, it almost broke him. His family had to make immediate cutbacks on their lifestyle. They have not had new clothes in over a year and have been unable to afford repairs to Astley Court. They even cut the staff down by half, including myself. They've done all they can to avoid ruin."

"Have they?" Rayne felt petty for asking that, but where she came from, a person had to work to earn his or her place. Marrying her seemed like an easy solution for Oliver, but not a fair one to her.

Ellen nodded. "Lord Conway came here not to celebrate Christmas, but to beg Lord Fraser as a family friend to offer him a position as an estate steward. Lord Fraser has a man in Inverness to handle his interests here, but he's been looking to hire a man in London."

"How do you know all of this?" Rayne asked.

"Before I was let go by Lord Conway, I heard he was planning to come here this Christmas with that goal in mind. He never meant to live off anyone's fortune. He planned to work, but the debt on Astley Court was too high, and he needed money quickly to save his family, as well as their home."

"Then he met me, and now he thinks he won't have to." Rayne knew she sounded spiteful, but clinging to her anger was the only way she could keep the sorrow from drowning her.

"I asked him what his intentions were toward you, and I told him he had to win your love. What does your heart tell you about him?"

Rayne could feel tears forming in her eyes again.

"Ellen, you don't understand. I will never know if it was me or my fortune. That is no way to start a marriage."

Ellen's gaze dropped to the floor as the coach stopped and they climbed out.

"Let's go purchase our tickets." Rayne headed toward the ticket office. She got to the front of the line, where a man with wire-rimmed spectacles reviewed the train timetables.

"Next train leaves in an hour and a half, miss."

"How much?" she asked.

"Ten shillings per ticket."

She removed the coins from her reticule and paid the ticket man. He filled out two ticket booklets and handed them to her.

She and Ellen went to the first-class refreshment room to wait. She didn't miss the way her maid looked at her from time to time, her lips parting, then closing again as if she wished to speak but dared not.

"Miss...," Ellen finally said.

"Yes?" A headache started behind Rayne's eyes, a dreaded pulse beating in a pounding rhythm that would make her sick before long if she could not banish it. She wanted to pretend the last few days had never happened.

If I had never met him, never shared a kiss, or a bed... If I had never fallen in love...

Could she truly regret falling in love? The moments she had shared with him, the heated kisses, the late-night whispers, reading beside each other, the feel of their bodies merging into one another, the stories of their pasts... She didn't want to forget any of that. But every minute she thought about it made it hard to breathe.

"Miss, sometimes life is a complicated thing. Love, great love, can exist, even when money is involved. You are beautiful, intelligent, and kind. A man like Lord Conway could easily fall in love with you. I worked in his household for seven years, and I know him well. The way he was with you... He's never been like that with anyone."

"What about Adelaide Berwick?"

Ellen scowled. "Lady Adelaide?"

"Yes, they were childhood sweethearts. They were supposed to marry before he found out about me."

"What nonsense," Ellen said, then blushed. "Forgive me, miss. But Adelaide was a mere girl when Lord Conway was already a young man. She had calf eyes for him, but she was always a child to him. And she hurt Lady Zadie's feelings more than once, playing terrible pranks on her. If he was to marry her, it would be out of desperation for his family and his home. He loves Astley Court."

Rayne recalled how he had spoken of Astley with a fondness that warmed his eyes. He had spoken of a home and sharing his with her. She had been enchanted by the idea. A home special enough to truly belong to her had always been her heart's secret desire, right after finding a man who loved her for herself and not her fortune. All of Oliver's stories of Astley had seemed like fate. But now those sunny feelings were overshadowed by his deception.

"Why did he lie, Ellen? Why not tell me the truth from the start?"

Her maid met her gaze. "Would you have given him a proper chance? Any man paying court to you would realize soon enough that you wouldn't marry except for love, and you would avoid any man who looked even a little desperate. Not that anyone could blame you for such caution, but it would put him in a bit of a bind."

Rayne wanted to deny it, but she couldn't. Ellen spoke the truth. Rayne would have sent him on his way the moment she learned he needed a fortune for his home and family.

"He still lied to me," she said, though with less conviction.

"He did," Ellen agreed. "But given his motives, that doesn't make him a terrible person. When he spoke to me about you, he didn't want to deceive you. He's not a man seeking money for his own selfish desires, nor is he a man prone to vices. His needs are selfless."

"I so badly want to believe that what we shared was real..." Fresh tears trailed down her cheeks.

Ellen handed her a handkerchief. "It might have been, but you left before you could know for certain. Love sometimes requires a leap of faith."

A passage came back to her from Oliver's book, *The Black Arrow*.

"He began to understand what a wild game we play in life; he began to understand that a thing once done cannot be undone nor changed by saying 'I am sorry.'"

Could she forgive Oliver? Could she still go forward and see if what they had between them was truly love?

"Our train leaves in twenty minutes," Ellen said quietly. "We should board."

Rayne rose from her seat in the refreshment room, and they headed toward the waiting train. But each step seemed to become harder and harder, as an invisible pull tried to keep her here in Inverness, with Oliver.

OLIVER EXITED LORD FRASER'S STUDY, HIS HEART beating in excitement. Fraser had agreed to give him the London steward position. It would pay decently the first year, and if Fraser found his work satisfactory, he would receive a 25 percent wage increase the following year. It would be enough to keep his family in a small but decent townhouse in London. He had resigned himself to losing Astley Court and everything within its walls, but if it meant he kept Rayne as his wife, he would give up whatever was necessary.

After seeing her so upset today, seeing how he had hurt her beyond imagining with his deception, he knew he would do anything to keep her, to make her happy and love her. She was a gift more valuable than any manor house, more valuable than anything aside from his family. And he wanted her to be part of that family. He was going to win her back.

He entered the billiard room, where several gentlemen were drinking and talking, including Mr. Egerton.

"Ah, Conway," Douglas greeted him. "Join us for a drink?"

"Actually, Mr. Egerton, I wonder if I might speak to you?"

"Of course." Douglas followed him out of the billiard room and into the room across the hall, which happened to be the library.

He got straight to the point, knowing that Rayne's father preferred that. "Mr. Egerton, I have asked Rayne to marry me."

"And you need my blessing?"

"Well, it's more complicated than that, I'm afraid. I need your help." He drew in a breath to steel his nerves.

"Complicated?"

"Yes. You see, I wasn't entirely honest with Rayne. My family is destitute. My father made a number of ill-fated investments before his death, and they put us into debt. I spent over a year cutting down expenses and selling much of what we own, but it isn't enough. I came to Lady Poole's ball intending to propose to Lady Adelaide Berwick."

Douglas's gaze was stormy, but he continued to listen.

"Then I met Rayne, and everything was so perfect

—*she* was perfect. I didn't even know who she was when I met her. I learned her name only after I left the ball. My sister, Zadie, had also met her and knew that she was..."

"An heiress?" Douglas supplied quietly.

Oliver swallowed. "Yes. I knew then that she was the one I wished to marry. I didn't tell Rayne about my family's financial situation. I should have, but I didn't."

"Does she know now?" Douglas asked.

Oliver nodded. "And she refuses to speak to me."

Rayne's father crossed his arms. "So you want me to change her mind and get her to take you back? I won't do that."

"No, that isn't—"

"You listen to me, Conway. I know all about American heiresses who buy titled husbands, but my daughter doesn't want a title. She wants love, like her mother. I will write a check for whatever amount you need to walk away. Her heart will be broken, but at least she will be free."

"A check?" Oliver echoed in confusion.

"Yes." Douglas's tone was brusque. "I can easily pay off whatever debts you owe. But once I do, that's the end. You leave her alone."

Oliver's stomach knotted with nausea. He'd come to Douglas for help, not money.

"Mr. Egerton, I don't want even a sixpence of Rayne's fortune. That's what I came to tell you. I want Rayne. Nothing else. I came here to ask you to draw up a settlement that gives Rayne an allowance but restricts me as her husband from using any of it. Leave your fortune to your brother and his sons. I want none of it —I only want her."

"You..." Douglas frowned as he tilted his head to one side. "You would give up millions of pounds to marry my daughter?"

"I intend to give up *everything*, including my home."

"So how will you support yourself and her if you don't have her fortune?"

"A few weeks before I met Rayne, I had plans to come here for the holidays to meet with Lord Fraser about employment with him. He needs a London steward for his property holdings. He has agreed to give me the position. If I do well the first year, he'll raise my wages by quite a significant amount. So long as Rayne is comfortable with a modest townhouse in London, I can support her, and she may use her allowance from you however she likes, with no interference from me."

"Do you know anything about managing property?" There was a subtle challenge in his question.

"I do. I may be a titled lord, but we do learn how to manage our estates starting at a young age. Some better than others. My father wasn't the most skilled, but I believe I am well suited for it."

"Hmm..." Douglas still had his arms crossed. "What if you agree to this and then change your mind?"

"That's where the settlement comes in. I thought we

could draft it today and execute it before witnesses so there's no doubt as to my intentions."

"If you intend to trick me, Conway..."

"It's no trick," Oliver assured him. "I made a mistake by believing that life would bless me and my family twice with both love and money, but love is the only thing that *truly* matters. I was a fool not to see this before. Losing Rayne's trust today made me realize that I cannot live without her, and all the money in the world is a poor companion when a man loses out on love."

"How could you fall in love with my daughter in only a handful of days?" Douglas leaned back against the nearest reading table.

"She shared her heart with me from the moment we met. She held nothing of herself back from me. And everything about her feels like a miracle to me. A beautiful miracle. Her smile, her laugh, her wit, her compassion, and her bravery. She is a woman who lives to be loved. And it would be my greatest honor to be that man, if she'll still have me."

"You think that this settlement you propose will mend her broken heart? Or will she see it only as the start of another deception?"

Oliver curled his hands into fists at his sides, trying to control his desperation for Douglas to understand. He met the man's eyes with a steady gaze and unwavering words.

"I don't know, but I have to try. What we share isn't

ordinary, and I need to prove to her that I will fight to win her trust back."

Douglas was silent a long moment, and for a second Oliver feared that he wouldn't help.

"Come, we'll have the paperwork drafted and witnessed. Then you can find Rayne and try to change her mind."

They got permission from Lord Fraser to use his study to draft the settlement. Once it was executed and a copy was made, Oliver carried the copy rolled up and bound with a ribbon. He went straight to Rayne's room. A maid was inside, tidying up the bed.

"Excuse me, do you know where Miss Egerton is?"

"She left, my lord." The maid bent over the bed, tucking in the sheets tight.

"Left?" Oliver choked out the word.

"Yes." The maid pulled a pair of letters from her pocket and handed them to him. One was addressed to Lord Fraser and the other to her father.

A terrible numbness settled inside Oliver's chest as he carried the letters downstairs. He summoned Lord Fraser and Mr. Egerton to the hall to deliver the notes.

"What's all this?" Fraser said as he scanned its contents. "Egerton, your daughter is headed to London?"

Douglas opened his letter, which was much longer. "She's leaving from the Inverness train station and plans to wait for me in London. I apologize, Lord Fraser, for her rude departure."

"That's fine. Is the lass all right?" Fraser asked, his gaze shooting between Douglas and Oliver.

"I believe so," Douglas sighed. "Just a bit of a broken heart."

"Lord Fraser, may I borrow a horse?" Oliver cut in.

"Yes, of course." The Scottish lord's eyes narrowed. "You're going after her?"

Oliver nodded. "Her leaving was my fault."

"Ah. Then you'd best go now, Conway. There are several trains to London a day—you could miss her." Fraser sent him a meaningful look, and Oliver returned it. Fraser had loved a woman and lost her, so he knew what that felt like. It was a pain like no other, and he didn't wish it upon any man.

Oliver didn't hesitate. He ran for the door, the settlement tucked firmly in his coat. He couldn't let Rayne go, not without trying everything in his power to get her back.

"Godspeed, lad!" Fraser shouted as he rushed into the cold winter air.

I need one Christmas miracle. Please let me reach her in time.

❦ 12 ❦

Rayne stood on the platform, watching the attendants load her and Ellen's luggage into the luggage compartment. They had twenty minutes still until the train left the Inverness station. Ellen stood beside her.

"Are you sure you want to leave?"

"I can't stay. Seeing him there for another week? I'm not sure my heart could take it." Rayne closed her eyes and then drew a deep breath. "Let's go ahead and board." They took their seats in the first-class compartment.

She stared unseeing out the windows. "I feel like I see him everywhere, Ellen. I see him, I hear him..." Would she ever escape the memories that were guaranteed to break her heart over and over?

"Rayne!" The memory of Oliver's voice intruded on

her thoughts. She blinked away tears as she stared out the train windows.

Steam billowed up, casting shadows as figures moved onto the platform and sunlight shone down to the station's tall glass windows. It was a strange blend of worlds, the shadowy station and fierce, gleaming black-and-red engines momentarily illuminated by shafts of sunlight before they were swallowed up again by clouds of smoke and steam.

"Rayne!" The shout came again, and she sat up a little straighter as she realized someone *was* calling her name.

"Miss..." Ellen pointed at a figure half-shrouded in steam.

Oliver. He was here and running down the length of the train platform, calling her name. Unable to resist, she leaned against the glass as he approached her compartment window.

"Ray—" He stopped, staring at her. Then he rushed down to the first-class car's door and attempted to board the train, but two attendants held him back. They gripped him by his arms and dragged him away so he couldn't get inside.

"Rayne! Please, just let me speak to you!" he shouted through the window. Desperation marred his features, and it made her inner resolve to ignore him quake and shudder until it was on the verge of collapsing.

"I think you should listen to him, miss," Ellen said. "Otherwise, you'll always be wondering what he came all this way to say that wasn't already said. You still have fifteen minutes before the train departs."

Rayne nodded and, hands shaking, stood and left her compartment. Soon she and Oliver stood on the platform half a dozen feet apart, neither daring to breathe.

"Please... There's something I have to say. Then if you still want to leave, I won't stop you." He reached into his coat and pulled out a piece of ribbon-bound paper. "Read this."

She stepped toward him and collected it, carefully removing the ribbon. After she unrolled the paper, she read the words on the page, words she knew her father had written because she recognized his handwriting. It stated that Oliver would receive no money from their marriage and that she would have a livable sum each month provided by a trustee that Oliver could not use.

She looked up at Oliver, confused. Did he really mean to take her without her fortune?

"Oliver, why did you sign this?" she asked, her voice shaking. "Did my father make you?"

"No. I signed it because I love you. If that means giving up everything else, then it is an easy choice. You are the *only* thing that matters to me." There was no hesitation in him as he spoke.

"But what about your home and your family?"

"I cannot save Astley Court without paying off a large portion of the debt by the middle of January. Lord Fraser has given me his London steward position, and I will earn enough to support both you and my family, but the money I earn wouldn't be enough to pay what's currently owed to keep Astley. However, we will be able to have a decent townhouse in London. We shall live frugally for a time, but well enough that there should be no shame in it."

Now he hesitated. "I wasn't honest with you from the beginning, at least not about my financial situation. Everything else about me, everything that we shared, was real. I would never lie to you again, not even a lie of omission, if you still wanted to be my wife..." He raked a hand through his hair and chuckled wryly. "I'm bungling this up, I know that, but the point I'm trying to make is that I adore you, Rayne, and I would give everything to call you my wife."

Rayne bit her lip as a dozen conflicting emotions battled for dominance. The train conductor blew the whistle and called out that there were ten minutes left to board.

She looked down at the settlement. "I..." If she wanted more concrete proof that he loved her for herself and not her fortune, there was nothing better than the document she held in her hands. It was already signed and executed. That meant her father must have believed Oliver, and that bolstered her own desire to trust him again.

She closed her eyes and listened to her heart. She had loved Oliver from the moment he had come into Lady Poole's library, a mysterious dark-haired prince from some fairy tale. When she opened her eyes, she handed the legal document back to him, and the look of hurt in his eyes almost broke her. He thought he had lost her. She stepped up to him and curled her gloved hands around his coat lapels, pulling him close.

"Yes."

His green eyes lit with a hope that burned so brightly it almost made her cry.

He wound one arm around her waist. "Yes?"

She nodded and buried her face against his chest. "Yes."

He pressed his lips against her forehead and the crown of her hair, murmuring sweet promises that melted her heart because she knew Oliver would keep them.

"Oh!" She pulled back suddenly. "My luggage!" She spun away from him to hurry to the luggage car, but she halted just as quickly. Ellen stood a dozen feet away, a stack of traveling cases already at her feet.

"Ellen, how did you...?"

Her maid grinned. "I told you Lord Conway was a good man. I believed he would make things right, so I went to fetch our luggage."

Rayne rushed to embrace her maid and whispered a heartfelt thanks to her.

"It'll be nice to work for the Conway family again," Ellen said as Oliver waved to a station attendant to help take their luggage. They would need to hire a coach, since Lord Fraser's coach had to be on its way back to the estate by now.

Once they were all seated, Rayne leaned against Oliver's side and tucked her arm in one of his. He rested his cheek on top of her head.

"Thank you," he whispered.

She lifted her head to look up at him. "For what?"

"For saving me from a life I would've regretted. That night we met, I was going to propose to Adelaide. I lost the courage and went to the library and found you. I thought we would never see each other again, but meeting you showed me what I really wanted in life. I wanted love, a real connection."

Rayne kissed him softly, her lips trembling. "Thank you for loving me, Oliver. After losing my mother, I have felt so alone, and you came into my life, lighting up the night sky like a shooting star."

She pressed her cheek against his shoulder. His woolen coat and the gold fur around his collar tickled her when she stole another few kisses.

Ellen, bless her, pretended to focus on reading a book and not to see what they were doing.

By the time they returned to Lord Fraser's home, Rayne felt as though she could fly up the stairs from happiness alone. Oliver assisted both her and Ellen from the coach and escorted them inside.

Lord Fraser and her father were just inside, waiting for them.

"Ah, so you've returned with your fair lass?" Lord Fraser said to Oliver, but he winked at Rayne.

Oliver's face reddened. "I have." Then he looked to her father and held the settlement paper out to him. Her father took it, but he was more interested in searching his daughter's face for any sign of unhappiness. He didn't find any.

"You're truly happy, daughter?" her father murmured.

"Yes, ridiculously so."

"That's all a father can ask for." He let her go and shook Oliver's hand. "Welcome to the family."

"Thank you, Mr. Egerton."

"Douglas, please." Her father smiled mischievously. "Now, seeing as we've been missing most of the festivities..." He nodded toward the corridor behind them, where the boisterous sounds of people singing carols came from one of the parlors.

Rayne followed Oliver as they entered the room, and dozens of eyes swept their way. Adelaide saw them, and anger flashed across her face before she masked it behind cool, practiced indifference. But when Oliver's family saw them, they all broke into smiles.

"Do they know about the settlement?" Rayne asked Oliver. "Will they be angry?"

"Everett was the one who thought of it. I was falling apart and couldn't think past the pain of losing you, but he knew what to do. I owe him for that. I'm sure he's told Mother and Zadie."

"I hope so. I don't want your family to despise me."

Oliver laughed. "They're your family too, and they won't despise you. They'll adore you, just as I do." He looked at her seriously. "I want you and your father to come stay at Astley Court after Fraser's house party is over. We won't have it for much longer, and I want to show it to you." He clasped her hands in his. "And please understand that I am not attempting to coerce you into trying to save it. I just want to share it with you."

"I understand." She clasped his hands in return, and then they joined the others.

Someone sat down at the pianoforte, and Everett began to sing "God Rest Ye Merry, Gentlemen" in a deep baritone, and Oliver soon joined him. Rayne's heart swelled as she watched the pair of them singing. But she suddenly tensed as Adelaide sat down beside her.

"So, he won you back?" To Rayne's surprise, her tone was more puzzled than venomous.

Rayne gave her a wary look. "Yes."

"How? Did you change your mind about the money?"

"No. *He* changed his mind. He decided I mattered more to him than his home. He went to my father and had a settlement drafted that gives him nothing. I will live on a small allowance."

Adelaide's Cupid's bow mouth parted in shock. "He truly did that?"

"He did." Rayne would have celebrated her victory, but something about Adelaide seemed broken now. Or rather, the broken part of herself that had been well hidden until now was finally beginning to show.

"I always thought I'd be the one to marry him," Adelaide said, her eyes fixed on Oliver, and some of her bitterness seemed to fade as a deep pain etched itself in her features.

"Lady Adelaide... There is still hope for a woman who turns her heart toward kindness. Love finds a way."

Adelaide glared at her. "Is that your way of telling me to be nice to you?"

"Not to me, to *everyone*. Men—the ones worth marrying, anyway—are attracted to ladies with open and kind hearts. You can still be fierce and proud in your way, but you need not be so cruel to others." Part of Rayne was baffled that Adelaide was talking to her after everything that had happened, but she pitied the woman for her unrequited feelings toward Oliver. Peeking a glance back at Oliver and Everett, she noticed Everett watching them both, but he hastily glanced away.

Was it possible Everett was...interested in Adelaide?

"What about Everett? Would you ever consider...," Rayne suggested.

Adelaide snorted. "That devil? Certainly not. He used to tease me when we were younger. Left tadpoles in my teacups, tacks on my chair, always shoving me and pulling my hair. He and Zadie always laughed at me when they managed to get me into trouble."

"Oh…" Rayne shot a glance at Everett, who was casting them a covert glance again. "Sometimes a boy doesn't know how to express his affection."

"Oh, Everett certainly does with women he likes. I am not one of those women. There's no love lost between us, I assure you. He practically crowed at me earlier that Oliver was never going to marry me. He seemed quite happy at the thought." Adelaide lifted her chin and changed the subject. "Did you really have a whole wardrobe ordered from the House of Worth? I was too afraid to ask my father for even one dress."

"Yes. They are expensive, though not as much as one would imagine."

"Well… I shall look forward to seeing your ball gown this evening after dinner. Lord Fraser is having a small orchestra come in to play for the dance this evening." Adelaide stood and drifted away to speak to some other ladies, pretending nothing at all was wrong and acting like her usual judgmental self.

Zadie took her place in the chair Adelaide had vacated. "Goodness, that appeared quite civil from across the room. Was it?"

"Indeed it was, and I am just as surprised as you are."

"Whatever will be the next Christmas miracle?" Zadie asked with a giggle.

"I'd settle for a snowstorm that gives us a white Christmas."

"Perhaps we'll get lucky?" Zadie leaned in and hugged Rayne. "I'm so happy we are to be sisters."

"Me too," Rayne admitted, but she bit her lip. "I'm sorry I couldn't marry Oliver without the settlement."

"It's fine, Rayne. We'll manage. I will admit I was disappointed when I first heard about the arrangement, but then I asked myself what I would do if I were in your position. I couldn't see myself accepting anything less. And Oliver's happiness will always matter more to us than money."

Later, as the orchestra played and people danced, snow began to fall outside. Oliver claimed her for almost every dance. Her father and Lord Fraser had claimed the others, and Everett, the delightful scoundrel, had swept in and stolen one of Oliver's, carrying her off before his brother could intervene. But now she was back in Oliver's arms as they spun in a waltz. Her red-and-cream gown flowed behind her, and she used one hand to hold part of her silk train out away from herself so she could twirl in his arms.

"You are utterly captivating," Oliver said as he held her a bit too close, though no one judged him for it. They were to be married tomorrow morning. Her father and Lord Fraser had spoken to the local minister, and all had been arranged. Rayne couldn't have been happier; it felt like her entire body was full of bubbling champagne.

As the music finally ended and sleepy people headed upstairs for the night, Oliver escorted Rayne to her room and stole a soft kiss, but as Rayne opened her door, she grasped his jacket and pulled him inside with her.

"An early honeymoon?" he asked as he slipped out of his coat.

"Does that bother you?" She knew it didn't, because his eyes were bright and heated with desire.

"Not at all, so long as you are content with a wicked husband teaching you all the delights and the most sinful pleasures he knows."

"Oh, that sounds lovely." She gasped as he spun her to pin her against the closed door and they faced each other. She clung to his shoulders as he pushed up her gown and unfastened his trousers.

"With our clothes on?" she asked in a scandalized whisper.

Oliver nodded and then stole her mouth with his as he lifted one of her legs to wrap around his waist. He shifted her body up, and then he was inside her.

Rayne opened for him, his thrusts sending waves of pleasure through her. The intensity of their love-making built higher each time Oliver thrust deep. This wasn't about sweetness and slow passions—it was a moment of wild madness, the need to reconnect after what they'd almost lost. He kissed her neck, his warm breath sending tingles down her spine and making her even wetter. She came apart a moment later, her inner walls trying to hold him deep and never let him go.

Oliver gasped her name, almost crushing Rayne against the door as he tightened and released himself within her. He buried his face in her neck, kissing the shell of her ear as he held her upright, then gently set her down on her feet, her skirt falling back down. Her legs wobbled like one of the towering molded jellies served at dinner. Rayne giggled and squealed as Oliver swept her up and carried her to the bed. He stripped out of his clothes and then took his time removing hers inch by inch.

"Such a shame to strip you of that gown, but I want you naked, my love." He tucked her in bed and climbed in beside her, pulling her flush against him.

Rayne let out a yawn, then smiled in embarrassment, her cheeks hot.

"I'm sorry. I feel today I have lived a lifetime of emotions, and it's exhausted me." She laid a palm on his chest, the feel of his heartbeat a steady reassurance.

"You have, and it was my fault. I'm sorry I kept the truth from you. I won't ever do that again. You have my word."

"Thank you, Oliver. I know it is asking much of you to give up your home for me. I will do everything to make you happy," she promised.

Oliver lifted her hand to his lips, pressing a kiss to her knuckles. "I'm giving up Astley Court in exchange for the love of my life. I'm the one who owes *you* everything." He laced his fingers through hers. "You're my Christmas miracle, Rayne. Never doubt that, or my love for you. I'm only sorry that I'm not able to offer you a more lavish lifestyle."

She raised her head to look at him. "I've never needed that. Truth be told, I've never wanted it. I've only ever wanted love and a true home with a family that my father and I could be a part of."

Her future husband grinned down at her. "Those are presents I'm certain Saint Nicholas shall deliver." Then he kissed her, and she forgot all her worries. Only love remained. Outside, the snow continued to fall, blanketing the Scottish Highlands in a world of white.

RAYNE MARRIED OLIVER THE FOLLOWING MORNING, inside an old Norman church that had a dozen tall stained-glass windows framed within the stone walls. The morning light shone through and splashed colors upon the wooden pews. A dozen guests attended, but Rayne was barely aware of them. She stood beside Oliver in an ivory silk gown threaded with hundreds of pearls upon the sleeves and bodice. The colors from the stained glass played over her gown, making her glow. She felt like a princess, and she knew that wherever her mother was, she would have smiled right along with her.

"You look opalescent," Oliver said as he slipped a ring upon her finger. She trembled a little. Her body couldn't seem to contain her love, which was ready to burst out.

The minister cleared his throat, and Oliver wiped the smile off his face as they continued their vows. Rayne wanted to memorize this moment. The fresh smell of lilies at the base of the altar, the flickering candles in their tall silver holders, the feel of Oliver's hand on hers. How strange and wondrous it all was to marry the mysterious man from Lady Poole's library. Now she understood the shadows that had lingered in his eyes that night as he had to say goodbye. She couldn't help but think perhaps her mother had been there, a guiding spirit trying to bring two lonely hearts together, binding them by books and candlelight in the sanctuary of a library.

All shadows and doubts were gone now, however. There was only love and trust. They shared a kiss as they were declared husband and wife. And then everything was a blur of laughter and smiles, even a few tears as she and Oliver took a coach back to Lord Fraser's home, where they continued the celebration with a wedding breakfast.

Lord Fraser stood up and called for his guests' attention. "If you've all had enough cake, I'd like to initiate a challenge for you to join me outside."

"In the snow?" someone asked.

Lord Fraser nodded. "Precisely." Fraser shot Oliver a wink, which Oliver returned.

Rayne curled her hand around Oliver's arm, leaning in to whisper, "Is this what I think it is?"

"It is. And I challenge you, my love, to a snowball fight. Now go and change into something warm and meet me outside."

Rayne, Zadie, and half a dozen other ladies rushed upstairs to change. Rayne came back down wearing a bustled red velvet gown and sturdy black boots, ready for battle. The men had already started, pelting balls at one another, and when they spotted the ladies, they quickly joined forces and turned on them. Rayne ran at the men, throwing as many as she could manage, until she slipped on a patch of ice. Oliver caught her in his arms, shielding her from the next snowball like the gallant knight he was. He kissed her soundly, and when he pulled back, she smacked him with a powdery handful of snow.

"Minx!" He let her go to wipe his face, and she dashed away across the lawn.

Snow began to fall in tufts like bits of cotton, and Oliver came after her again, unarmed.

"Mercy, my dear lady, mercy." He held up his hands in surrender. The snow dappled his navy-blue woolen coat and dark hair. She flung herself at him, and he caught her by the waist, spinning them both around in a cloud of swirling snowflakes.

"Thank you for forgiving me," Oliver breathed, holding her close as they spun to a stop. "Thank you."

The tight warmth of his embrace felt like a vow, one that could never be broken.

"We forgive those we love—it's what makes love the most powerful force in the world." She held him right back, letting him know they would always support one another.

"I won't ever deserve you, but I intend to spend the rest of my life trying to." Oliver gave her one of those kisses that melted upon her lips like sugar and lingered like the sweetest of wine. It was the way he stared at her afterward, as if she was indeed some kind of miracle.

She carried the memory of that look with her all the way to Christmas four days later.

After everyone had retired from the Christmas Day festivities, she and Oliver sat in bed, and he held out a velvet box to her.

"What is it?" she asked as she accepted it.

"It belonged to my great-grandmother, the Duchess of Essex. My mother was hoping I would find a bride soon, and this was something we both felt should belong to you. I hope you like it. It was one of the few things we couldn't bear to part with when we started selling much of our belonging this last year."

With shaky fingers, Rayne opened the box. A single strand of pearls lay there. They gleamed in the firelight with perfect shape and color.

"They're beautiful." She touched the silky pearls, listening to them click against one another. She grinned mischievously. "Are they cursed like the Koh-i-noor diamond?"

Oliver raised a brow in a mockingly serious expression. "*Terribly* cursed. Whoever wears them must suffer a thousand kisses before midnight."

Rayne fell back into the mountain of pillows as Oliver began to unleash that curse. But soon the kisses deepened, and she sighed in delight as he covered her body with his.

A long while later, Rayne slipped out of bed and put on her nightgown. She left Oliver in bed and went over to the traveling cases he had moved into her room. She dug through the contents of one case until she found the settlement agreement.

"Rayne?" Oliver muttered drowsily as he stirred in the bed. "Come back here, love."

She returned to the bed but did not climb in. She held the agreement in front of her and played with the ends of the black ribbon.

"I have a present for you too." She turned away and approached the fireplace. He sat up in bed, his eyes wide.

"Rayne, what are you doing?" He started to leave the bed, but she was too fast and flung the settlement into the fire.

Oliver grabbed his dressing gown and pulled it on before he joined her at the fire to watch it burn.

"I know my father has a second copy, but I wanted

you to see this. I changed my mind. I want to share my fortune with you. I want... I want to save our home."

"You've never even seen Astley Court," Oliver replied as he placed his hands on her waist and drew her back against him while they watched the paper burn.

"You love it. That's all that matters. You once told me that people should be able to lean on others for support. I thought you wanting my money was selfish, but I love you and it will be my home too. So that means I can be selfish and save Astley Court. The best way to do it is to undo the settlement."

Oliver held her close, his voice slightly rougher than before when he said, "I would never ask you to do this. I didn't want there to ever be a doubt I chose only you."

"I don't doubt you, Oliver." She turned in his arms. "You need to trust me now. Trust that I want this for us."

His green eyes were overbright as he nodded and kissed her. "I suppose miracles really do happen, don't they?"

Rayne brushed a lock of hair out of his eyes. "They certainly do. Especially when one makes one's own miracles." She grinned.

Oliver chuckled, and then he lowered his head to steal another kiss. "Happy Christmas, my love."

"*Merry* Christmas," she corrected with a laugh.

"You Americans." He swept her up into his arms and carried her back to bed.

EPILOGUE

T<i>en months later</i>
A crisp fall wind blew red and gold leaves across the path that led up to Astley Court. Everett shoved his hands into his coat pockets as he moved up the cobblestone walkway. The towering rhododendrons nearly walled him off from the front gardens and kept his path concealed from anyone who might be waiting for him at the house. He was already running late for afternoon tea, and his mother would no doubt give him an earful.

A feminine voice gasped somewhere around the bend. "Ouch!"

Everett quickened his pace and followed the sound. He burst into the clearing around the bend, expecting to see his sister or perhaps his sister-in-law, but instead he found Adelaide Berwick. She was the last person he would ever have wanted to run into, especially alone in a garden. Perched on the marble bench, dressed in a bustled green satin gown, clutching her hand, Adelaide painted a pretty portrait of a damsel in distress, not that he was attracted to that sort of thing. He *definitely* wasn't.

"Adelaide?"

She jerked as he spoke her name, dropping a rose bloom to the ground in her haste. Given how close their families' properties were, it wasn't unusual to see Adelaide stray into the family gardens, just as he'd often hopped the low stone wall to go fishing in the little lake on Adelaide's land.

"Oh!" She rose from the bench to flee, but Everett caught her arm.

"What's the matter?"

"As if you cared," Adelaide snapped.

Everett saw a droplet of blood bead upon her fingertip. "So, you've learned you're not the only thing in the garden with thorns," he quipped, unable to help himself.

Adelaide's face twisted with a scowl as she pulled her hand free.

"Come now, I was only joking. Here, let me see." He caught her hand again and removed a handkerchief from his pocket. He pressed it to the pad of her right index finger and held it firm. They both stood silent a long moment. The heavy scents of late-blooming flowers mixed with the bite of an autumn wind stirring the golden trees around them wove a strange spell over

Everett as he studied Adelaide's face. For a moment she lost that cold, hateful look, and there was a softness there that puzzled him.

"What are you doing here?" Everett asked.

"I wanted a few roses. The ones in our hothouse at home don't have that..." She struggled for the right words. "Well, it's a wild look, an untamed beauty that our roses don't have. I didn't think you would miss the ones I took."

"And why do you need to poach our roses?" Everett still held on to her hand, the handkerchief wrapped around her finger.

The openness of her expression vanished. "You'll only laugh at me."

Everett wanted to disagree, but in the past, he had found reasons to tease Adelaide. She was such a prickly little creature.

"I almost certainly will, but tell me anyway."

"I wanted to sew a few roses into my gown for tonight's ball." Her face reddened like a ripe strawberry at the admission. Her auburn curls gleamed in the dappled sunlight as she turned her face away from his. To his own surprise, he didn't laugh.

"Ah, I understand. You wanted to have a gown like Rayne's from last Christmas?" he guessed. His sister-in-law had worn an exquisite gown with actual blooming roses sewn into it for one night. It had caused quite a stir among the guests.

"I... No," Adelaide huffed.

He moved one hand to her waist, rubbing his fingertips along her corseted form. He'd never noticed how much her body curved before, and how it felt strangely exciting to be touching her like this. "You don't need fresh roses, Adelaide. You're lovely as you are."

"*Just* lovely?" Her brown eyes darkened with seeming despair.

"Lovely isn't enough?" Everett rolled his eyes. "You're bloody exquisite. There, are you content now, Maddie?" He used the old nickname he'd teased her with as a child. She hated that name, but that was the point. He wanted to see fire in her eyes, not sorrow.

She smacked his chest and tried to pull away. "You callous bully! Don't ever call me that!" He'd taken to calling her Maddie Addie because he used to tease her for being madly in love with Oliver. Then it had somehow along the way shortened to just Maddie, but she still hated it.

Adelaide stared up at him, fire flashing in her eyes, and something just...changed between them in an instant. Like a flash of lightning from a building storm.

Unsure of what possessed him, Everett pulled her against his body and captured her lips. Her hiss of indignation changed to a confused gasp and then softened to a sigh of longing. He absorbed it all, fascinated by her sweet taste. He had never kissed her before, not once, and now he deeply regretted that. This was a woman who ought to be kissed a thousand times a day. Her petal-soft lips were made for sweet seductions, and the slight curve of her spine left his hand resting perfectly on her lower back while he enjoyed the press of her breasts against his chest. Lord, he could have stayed right there and kissed her for days.

He wasn't sure why they finally broke apart, but suddenly she was rushing away. Then she stopped, looking over her shoulder at him, the train of her green gown rustling over the fallen leaves. She looked like a startled wood nymph, and he wanted her back in his arms.

That was madness. He was the mad one, not her. She was *Adelaide*, the spoiled little rich girl who lived next door. The girl who'd followed his older brother about with big doe eyes and never looked his way, not even once. He despised her... Didn't he? Then she was gone, vanishing down a garden path back to her estate. Everett stared at the leafy rhododendrons for a long second and then resumed his walk back to Astley Court.

"Everett!" Rayne and Oliver called out his name in unison as he came up the steps. Rayne held a bundle of cooing joy in her arms. A little boy born only a month before. Justin Conway, the future Viscount Conway.

"Sorry I'm late." Everett held out his hands. "Now, let me see the little fellow." He took the babe from Rayne's arms and grinned down at him. Justin stared up at his uncle with a serious expression, his green eyes focused intently on Everett and his tiny brow furrowed.

"Hello there, old chap," he teased, then looked at the new parents. "How is everyone?"

"Wonderful," Oliver said. "Douglas and Lady Poole just arrived. Everything is set for their wedding this afternoon."

"Excellent." Everett hadn't been the least bit surprised to learn that Rayne's father and Lady Poole had formed an attachment. They were both bighearted and well suited to one another. After Rayne and Oliver had married, Rayne's father had decided to stay in London and not return immediately to New York, and naturally, he'd been pulled into Lady Poole's social activities, which had led to the widow and the widower falling in love.

"Are Zadie and Mother here?" Everett asked.

"Already inside," said Rayne. "Zadie is fending off the attentions of my cousins. They all seem quite taken with her."

"They do?" Everett narrowed his eyes. "Need we worry, Oliver?"

Oliver shook his head with a mirthful laugh. "Far from it. Zadie is holding court like a queen, and they've been fetching her tea and biscuits for the last hour. I believe they're ready to don the old suits of armor and ride out to battle for their fair lady's affection."

Everett snorted. Zadie did have a way of managing men when she wanted to.

"Margaret was surprised you weren't here first to eat all the sandwiches," Rayne teased. "I'm sorry there aren't many left. My cousins have almost eaten them all."

"Not to worry—Mrs. Mead always has a few tarts left in the kitchens for me."

Everett gave the baby one more loving squeeze and a smile before he slipped Justin into Oliver's waiting arms. Oliver stared down with bemused fascination at his son and then lifted the baby's impossibly tiny hand to his mouth and pressed a kiss to it. The sight tugged at Everett's chest. He had no desire to marry, at least not yet, but seeing Oliver so content, and embracing fatherhood in this way, made Everett long for the peace that had taken over his brother's life.

They entered the house, and Everett glanced once more toward the gardens in the direction of Berwick House. He could still taste Adelaide's lips, and a sudden longing tightened his chest.

I must be mad to want her.

Yet he couldn't forget that singular kiss. Something had changed in him, because he knew he would dream about her lips tonight. He would perhaps dream of a bit more than a kiss too, and that was a dangerous thing.

ADELAIDE REACHED HER HOME, STILL CLUTCHING THE white handkerchief. She unwound it from her fingers and studied the initials *E. C.* sewn into the fabric with deep blue thread and lined with gold. A single bright red dot marred its center. She pressed her throbbing finger to her lips but didn't taste any fresh blood.

She felt like such a fool. Picking roses to look more like Rayne... Why had she done that? She had been jealous, that's why. Rayne always managed to look perfect, in her gowns with fashionable new designs from the House of Worth in Paris. Most ladies like Adelaide wore more sensible and pretty English dresses, but not stunning or risqué like the Parisian Worth dresses.

It was no wonder Oliver had fallen for Rayne. Adelaide must have looked as common as the other ladies compared to the American beauty. That night she'd first met Rayne, she'd been green with envy. And so she had done what she'd always done—resorted to meanness. It was what her mother had taught her, to strike out first at those you fear. Hurt them before they hurt you. It had proven to be effective. But now? Now she was thinking over and over about what Rayne had said last Christmas, about choosing kindness, not cruelty.

Adelaide squared her shoulders and looked back across the lawns of Berwick House toward Astley Court. She couldn't banish the memory of Everett kissing her. Everett... A man she'd loathed since childhood. As an adult, he'd become tolerable to talk to when necessary, but... no.

"Little Maddie Addie, little Maddie Addie..." She could still hear him teasing her from their childhood.

How she hated that name. It seemed so silly and common. And Everett knew she hated that nickname.

He was a bullheaded, stubborn bully, but that kiss... That kiss had been like the most wonderful dream. Not that Adelaide knew much about kisses. This was only her second one after a kiss from a stable hand years ago when she'd been sixteen. There was no need to compare the two experiences. Everett's mouth had set fire to her blood and made her dizzy. Wasn't that how a good kiss was supposed to be?

But instead of it coming from a handsome, polite suitor holding a bouquet of rare flowers, it had come from Everett Conway. Life, it seemed, always found new ways to be cruel to her.

Adelaide brushed her fingers over her lips and closed her eyes, wishing she could forget the feel of his mouth, and yet also wishing that he had never stopped kissing her. She clutched the handkerchief to her chest. A smile stole over her lips, but it soon faltered.

She couldn't fall for Everett. She *wouldn't*. Because she'd vowed to hate him for the rest of her life. The man had made her childhood miserable, and one kiss wouldn't change that, no matter how wonderful it had been or how she was likely to dream about it and him tonight.

"Damn you, Everett," she muttered. "Damn you."

THANK YOU SO MUCH FOR READING *SEDUCING AN*

Heiress on a Train! I hope you loved Rayne and Oliver's whirlwind Victorian romance! If you haven't read my book *Wicked Designs* yet, you might want to check it out because it's the love story for Oliver's great-grandparents Godric and Emily!

Be sure to turn the page to read my exclusive author's historical note where can read a little more about cursed Indian diamonds, train engines and the haunting true history of the witchery in Edinburgh.

AUTHOR'S HISTORICAL NOTE

Sometimes a story takes you by surprise, and you never know what magical things will be uncovered. Rayne and Oliver's Victorian-set romance was a true delight and an adventure for me in ways I never imagined. Between cursed diamonds, rumbling train cars, and the haunting and seductive atmosphere of a witchery at the base of a castle, there was plenty for me to explore with the story and, more importantly, with history. Below I wish to share with you a bit about some of the fun things I researched while writing this book.

When Oliver and Rayne share their secluded moment in Lady Poole's library, he mentions his grandmother seeing the Koh-i-noor diamond during the Great Exhibition in 1851. This is in fact all true, right down to the description of the diamond's viewing and the fact that it was later cut down to a perfect shape at the direction of Prince Albert. It is also true that Queen

Victoria never felt fully comfortable wearing the cursed diamond, and its history is indeed shrouded in blood-shed and mystery going back centuries. And when Oliver mentions his grandmother saying that to gaze upon it was like looking into a black abyss, that is actually true as well. Accounts from viewers during the Great Exhibition mentioned that strange and eerie phenomenon while viewing the diamond. This was a scene that surprised me, as the characters themselves revealed the Koh-i-noor in all its haunted beauty as I wrote. Just as Oliver's Grandmother predicted, it did end up in a crown a few generations after Victoria died. It was even in the crown which rested on the coffin of Queen Elizabeth II's mother while she lay in state.

As for the train scenes, I hope you all enjoyed that! I found the Pullman sleeping cars and the discussion of first-class refreshment rooms to be rather interesting. The history of trains is an extension of the history of stagecoaches, which is why train cars were originally called *coaches*. Another fascinating tidbit of truth is that people did believe early on that riding on or even being near those terrible black engines belching smoke and fire would actually drive a person mad. There was also a belief that the vibrations of the train and the rhythm of it would send women into "hysterics," which was a silly Victorian way of describing sexual arousal for women. It was still widely believed by many that women could not experience pleasure during sex (yes, I laughed outright at this too and then sadly shook my head). Naturally, the idea of women traveling on trains wasn't seen positively for this "hysterical" effect, but later on, train travel actually proved to be quite liberating for women and was one of the few places where women traveling alone without men or chaperones was allowed. Trains, in a way, were quite a powerful force for the movement toward independence for women.

Rayne as an American heiress marrying an English lord in the late 1880s was quite a common thing. "Buying a title," as they called it, was a frequent thing. New York was flooded with oil money and other fortunes, while the English economy was weakening by comparison. The English Nobility were trying to maintain landed properties without selling the land. Men like Oliver were responsible for supporting local farmers and their families, but with the economy changing, that way of life wasn't surviving. Many landed gentry and titled lords lost their homes and were forced to sell their estates due to mounting debts. Therefore, many Englishmen were happy to chase American heiresses to save their homes and their families. Men like Rayne's father, Douglas, were, however, very clever in protecting their daughters through settlements with the husbands. Sometimes the Englishmen were successful in getting their money, sometimes not.

The bewitching setting of the Witchery by the Castle is indeed a real place! My one bit of fiction about the Witchery is that it didn't start operating as a hotel until 1976. However, the building, with its brooding

Jacobean atmosphere, has been there for several hundred years. The history that Oliver tells Rayne as to the building's usage is indeed true—it simply didn't become a place someone could stay as a hotel guest until the twentieth century. You can stay there today! So the next time you're in Scotland, you can stop by the Witchery by the Castle to dine at their restaurant, or you can spend the night in a room just like Rayne and Oliver did.

I hope you all enjoyed *Seducing an Heiress on a Train* as much as I enjoyed writing it, and I hope you liked the small historical details I worked in to enrich the story.

Happy reading, my lovelies!

Lauren Smith

Psst! Turn the page to read a three chapter sneak peek of *Tempted by a Rogue* where Jasper, a dashing naval officer writes letters to Gemma, a woman he's loved since they were children, but there's just one problem, he's pretending to be his best friend, James, a man who won Gemma's heart years ago and has every intention of breaking it... (You can also skip reading the excerpt and just buy it HERE!)

TEMPTED BY A ROGUE

MIDHURST, WEST SUSSEX - 1817

White and pink roses formed spots of striking color against the dense green hedges as Gemma Haverford walked through the gardens of her home. She let her fingertips touch the petals of the roses as she headed toward the center of the garden. Twilight was her favorite time of day. Birds began to quiet their singing, the sunlight softened, giving everything a soft glow. Gemma took a seat on a cool marble bench at the center of the maze of hedges and rosebushes. Her hands trembled as she smoothed out her skirts. She was anxious enough that her knees knocked together too, but she couldn't banish her nerves.

It wasn't every day that she wore her best gown, an almost sheer sky blue silk, for a secret garden rendezvous. Everything needed to be perfect. She'd gone to great effort to have her lady's maid tame the wild waves of her hair and help to slightly dampen her gown to cling better to her form, which bore only the veiled protection of a single filmy shift.

She had to look her best tonight. At twenty-five she was past the age where most women found it easy to marry. One of her distant cousins had callously remarked earlier that year that she was so far back on the shelf that she was collecting dust. Gemma, feeling a little too irritated at the remark, and having one too many cups of arrack punch, had sneezed at him as though he was the one covered in dust. Not her finest moment, she had nearly dissolved in a fit of unladylike giggles at his horrified expression when he'd struggled to find the handkerchief in his waistcoat to wipe his face.

There was a very good reason she hadn't married, but she couldn't tell anyone, not even her parents why she'd turned down more than one suitor over the years. For eleven years she had kept herself out of the hunt for husbands, believing, *knowing* that she would marry one man, James Randolph, her childhood sweetheart.

He and his best friend, Jasper Holland, had enlisted in His Majesty's Navy as young midshipman. James had been fourteen and Jasper, half a year older, had been fifteen. For eleven long years the two men had been gone, making their fortunes on the high seas, but now they set to return home, to marry and settle down. She'd not seen them in all that time, but she knew in her heart of hearts, that James was coming for her. His

letters to her had been steady and filled with reassur-
ances of his affection and his intent to marry her as
soon as he came home. And now it was time.

What would he be like after so many years? Had he
changed like she had? Grown taller, more muscular,
more handsome than the wild young man who'd dashed
off to sea? Would he be stern as a husband after
commanding men and war ships? Or would he be gentle
with her after so many hard years at sea, and want
nothing more than a quiet country life full of friends
and family within an easy walk of one's home? It was
what she'd always wanted. She'd never cared for London
and the fast pace of the city. She adored the country, the
birds, the green lands, the sheep, even the garden
parties that her neighbors threw often were an amusement she enjoyed. Would James want the same thing?

Gemma nibbled her bottom lip, glancing about the
gardens. Wisteria hung over trellises to the entrance of
this particular part of the garden, the thick blooms
almost like wildflowers strung on green vines over the
white painted wood. How lovely it was here tonight.
How perfect too. She couldn't resist smiling.

Just that morning she had received James's latest
letter, telling her he would seek her out in the gardens
tonight, for a private audience, away from the eyes of
parents and chaperones.

Tonight. The one word held such promise. Enclosed
in James's letter was a soft strip of black gauzy cloth
embroidered with silver stars. The letter instructed her

to wait until twilight, and then blindfold herself for his arrival because he wished to surprise her.

A wave of heat flooded her cheeks at the thought of being so vulnerable and alone with him in such a manner, but another part of her heated in strange, unfamiliar places. She knew meeting him here like this wasn't proper and if anyone found out, she'd be compromised. But this was James, her James. The man she trusted more than anyone else in the world, except for her father. The temptation to meet him here, even in secret, was irresistible.

What would he do when he came upon her? Remove the blindfold? He might touch her face, her hair, her neck...Gemma trailed her own fingertips over her neck, wondering how different it would feel to have a man's hands there, ones worn with callouses from years of working the ropes while tacking the sails of a great ship.

A shiver rippled through her and she hastily dropped her hands back to her lap, feeling a little foolish. It was so easy to get carried away when thinking of James. When she first read the portion of the letter that told her to meet him like this, being compromised was her first fear, but James was a good and noble man. He was not the sort to ruin a lady, especially not when he intended to marry in good standing.

Even though she had not seen him since he set off eleven years ago, she had faith that he would not damage her virtue with this garden rendezvous. He would be a gentleman, wouldn't he? Gemma was all too aware that she knew little of the hearts of men, or how deeply they could fall prey to their desires.

Perhaps I ought to go back inside and wait for him to call upon me tomorrow morning? That would be the proper thing, after all.

Proper yes, but she wanted to see James alone and didn't want to wait another moment, even one night. If she were to be caught in a position that sorely injured her reputation, well, her father would demand a marriage immediately, James would comply, and all would be well.

Yes, all would be well enough. We need to be married, and mayhap it matters little how the deed comes about?

Perhaps that was what James intended, a certainty of compromising her so he could ensure they would be married. It was indeed a little unorthodox, but that might be his intent. To conquer her like he'd conquered his enemies upon the seas, swiftly and surely. If that were the case, then he was certainly a rogue. Another little smile twisted her lips.

Am I to marry a rogue? Wouldn't that be... She giggled unable to stop herself from thinking of how wonderfully wicked that would be. It would be scandalous, but if it was James, he would be *her* rogue.

So with that reassuring thought, she pulled the blindfold out, carefully put it over her eyes, and tied it into a small bow at the back of her head. She fiddled with her hair, tugging the loose untamable ringlets a little so they coiled down against her neck. Mary, her maid had done her best to fix it, but they both knew it would always look a bit wild. James would have to forgive her for appearing a little unruly. At least her gown had turned out well.

With the blindfold secure, she found she could see the vague outline of shapes through the thin gauzy cloth but her eyes were, for the most part, shielded from any clearer perceptions. Gemma smoothed her gown again, shifting restlessly as her stomach flipped over and over inside her. What if James had met with some delay, for he was not *officially* due to arrive in Midhurst until tomorrow where he and Jasper would be toasted and celebrated at Lady Edith Greenley's country estate garden party.

Gravel suddenly crunched close by as someone trod along the garden path leading straight toward her. She held her breath, sitting very still. It had to be James. Her heart fluttered so wildly that her ribs hurt from the hammering beat.

JASPER HOLLAND CURSED FOR THE THOUSAND TIME AS he fumbled his way through the maze of the Haverford Gardens. It was a bloody mess, this whole situation. It was James who should be here, not him, yet he was the one who was trapped in the situation of compromising a thoroughly decent young lady because his best friend was acting like a cur. Straightening his blue naval coat around his waist, he took another right turn, facing a dead end.

"Who designed this damnable thing? I'll likely lose my way and be eaten by a Minotaur," he muttered, stumbled back and took a left down another path. Someone should have drawn him a map to this—

He heard a feminine giggle some distance away and halted. The sound was light, a little husky, and it had the strangest effect on him just then. He could almost picture a woman beneath him in bed, just as he was about to enter her and ride her to their mutual pleasure making that sound. It was the best sort of sound in the world and one he hadn't heard in a long time. On the sea, there were often chances to visit the docks when in port, and pay for a night at a brothel. James had done that often enough, but Jasper never liked it.

There was something sad about the painted faces and the quiet resigned looks of the prostitutes that betrayed the way they felt about the manner in which they earned their living. More than once Jasper would pay to simply talk to them and then leave for the night, unsatisfied. After that, he'd taken to staying on the ship, leaving James to cavort on his own.

It still amazed him that after all these years he and James were friends. Many men were separated at sea and went years without seeing anyone. Losing touch often resulted in friendships waning. However, that hadn't happened with him and James. They'd been assigned to the same frigate, the *HMS Neptune* as midshipmen after attending a naval college. They'd both been promoted to first lieutenants and by the time they were ready to leave service, they were both still on the same ship.

Due to the influx of men joining the service, the waiting list to be promoted to captain was extensive and neither he nor James had enough peerage connections to curry favor for a quicker rise in officer status. Ergo they'd both agreed the time was good enough to leave service and return home. James had always been a bit of a rakehell, even as a young man before they'd left for the sea, but time had hardened both him and Jasper in different ways. He'd been more hesitant than Jasper to return to Midhurst and even the day before was talking about moving to London once he'd selected a pretty wife, one he could easily tire of and take mistresses later if he so chose. London was much better for mistresses than a little town like Midhurst.

"Love is for fools. Lust is what keeps a man going."

It was something James always said, something he'd taken to believing after so many years at sea. The women in ports had turned James into a jaded man and he'd abandoned dreams of marrying Gemma Haverford, the sweet little country gentleman's daughter he'd left behind.

"Jas, do a man a favor, write Gemma and break it off," he sneered under his breath in imitation of James's plea all those years ago.

It had started out so simple. A favor for a friend.

"And I'm the fool who took over writing those bloody love letters," Jasper growled in self-directed frustration.

He'd written one letter to Gemma, doing his best to imitate James's poor handwriting, but the words to end things...well they just hadn't come out on the page. Instead he found himself sharing details of his day, thoughts and impressions he had of the islands they'd visited, the strange lands and natives they'd encountered, the battles they'd faced. His fears, his hopes, his own dreams. And he'd signed that first letter with a single letter J. Not as James, but Jasper, the man he was. He hadn't wanted to deceive her any more than he had to. Her response to his first letter had been almost immediate. A letter back to him found him so quickly through the post that he had to assume she'd written it the second she'd received his letter.

The Gemma he'd met through her letters had fascinated him, amused him, and changed the way he thought of Midhurst. The little girl with ginger hair had changed so much. She'd become a woman worth knowing. Her stories and descriptions of the town, the village, the countryside, everything that was so easy to forget at sea, had kept him grounded and reminded him of home. It was no longer a place he'd escaped from to live a life of adventure, but become a wonderful place of refuge for him, a sanctuary to someday return to when his service was over.

But the game was now at an end.

James had found out on their last week aboard ship that Jasper hadn't broken off the secret engagement and that he'd continued to write to Gemma for the last ten years. James had been furious to learn that Gemma was now fully under the impression James was going to propose to her and that she'd saved herself for him and him alone. Jasper had read every letter where she'd detailed the passing London Seasons and how she'd felt a little pressured to marry, but had insisted she loved him and would wait. For James. Not him. The thought summoned a black cloud over Jasper's thoughts, but it wasn't going to change what he had to do tonight. He had to end it with Gemma while pretending to be James. Compromise her so that tomorrow morning when she met with James, he could discover she'd kissed another man and break it off with her forever.

Yes, it would ruin her, but Jasper had every intent of making things right, of marrying her himself. He would just have to convince her of that once the dust settled from James crying off. Jasper could wait, *would* wait for as long as he had to for Gemma to be his wife, his lover, his world. His only fear was that she would despise him for his deception all these years, but it was a risk he would have to take. He'd led her to believe he would marry her in his letters and he'd meant every word. If only he hadn't hidden behind the facade of being James.

I should have confessed my identity from the start, before I wove this tangled web, but 'tis too late now.

A bitter taste coated his tongue. Scowling, he peered through the nearest bush. He could just make out a feminine figure seated on a bench. It was a sight he'd never forget. The woman was lovely. She had a full figure, hips just the right size for a man's hands, and the perfect indent of a narrow waist. From where he stood, he couldn't see her front, but the twilight highlighted the riotous ginger colored waves of her hair that were escaping the nest of pins atop her head. She looked like a delicious little minx ready for a tumble into the nearest bed.

Lord, he wanted to be the man to take her to bed, to explore Gemma in a way he'd only fantasized about for years. Of course that had been purely dreams, he hadn't thought she'd look so tempting in real life. He remembered the little ginger-haired girl that had followed him and James about when they were children. He'd never had much interest in girls, but James had rather enjoyed the way she'd gazed at him with those sweet calf eyes. Adoration, no matter where the source came from had always been something James enjoyed and it had been only too easy for him to woo little Gemma with his smiles and teasing. Jasper had been far too busy to deal with girls at that age, he'd been more interested in exploring the hills and forests of Midhurst and getting in the sort of trouble boys were prone to do.

The woman on the bench sighed touched the blindfold over her eyes. It was made from a strip of cloth he'd found just for her in a little shop in a seaside port only a week ago. It was to be his tool of deception, a way to keep her from seeing him clearly, so she'd look back upon tonight and have to admit it was not James who'd visited her. It was a cruel plan. James's plan, not his, but Jasper was equally a bastard for going along with it.

"Hellfire and damnation," he muttered, squared his shoulders and walked around the nearest hedge. The time to compromise an innocent lady had arrived and he couldn't put it off another moment.

Forgive me, sweet Gemma.

CHAPTER 2

"James? Is that you?" She called out, her heart beating wildly with the excitement of the moment.

Her face warmed with the heat of a blush when she heard a soft intake of breath a few feet behind her. This moment was a decade in the making. She had dreamed of this deep into the night, and she could scarcely breathe with the abundance of joy inside her. Every letter, every anxious day waiting for a messenger to bring her news of him, had finally led to this night. Her life could begin again, this time with James by her side.

"Good god, is that you, Gemma? What a glorious creature you've grown up to be!" a low masculine voice uttered breathlessly.

It was curious, she had expected to recognize his voice, to hear it be just the same as the boy's voice she had carved into her memory, but it was not. The voice that spoke was that of a man, changed to a rich baritone, which rumbled sensually from behind her. She started to turn around on the bench but suddenly a body sat down behind her, arms circling her waist and lips brushing against her ear.

"Don't turn around," he whispered. "I want to see you like this, drink in my fill of you."

The shock of that intimate caress of his lips against her ear sent her jerking forward in panic. Sparks of sharp heat shot down between her thighs. Gemma tried to wrest herself free of his grasp because the way he held her made her feel so...queer.

"James, wait, I want to see you." Her hands flew to her face to remove the blindfold and get a glimpse of him. James, however, had other ideas. He snagged her arms, securing them at her sides as he jerked her back down against his lap on the marble bench. That forced closeness shot her heart into her throat and made her lightheaded with an unsettling mixture of emotions and physical awareness. He was a little rough, but rather than frighten her, it heightened her awareness of his strength. He touched the bare skin of her arms with his calloused palms.

Why didn't I wear gloves? A lady always wears gloves. But she hadn't tonight because she'd wanted to feel him, to touch him without a layer of silk between her fingers and his skin. Now she felt a skin to skin sensation, perfect, arousing. Arousing... yes that's what she felt.

Arousal. Mary had explained it to her in whispered tones when preparing her for tonight, she'd explained a kiss could do strange things to a woman's body if the man were skilled. It seemed Mary had been right.

James's arms tightened about her body to keep her from escaping, now were tight in an entirely different way. His breath turned heavy and he snuggled up to her.

"James, what are you doing?" She gasped, trying to pull free again.

"Shh...be still my lovely Gemma, embrace this twilight dream with me..." The words were honey smooth and delivered in such a perfect poetic cadence that Gemma was too entranced by the romance of it, to bother fighting off the amorous embrace of her love.

This was the man from the letters, the one who wooed with his words. Now he wooed her with his hands. She found it easy to relax beneath that soothing voice despite the clearly compromising position of her body fully against his. If no one came upon them, her reputation would be safe enough.

"It is good to hear your voice again, eleven years is such a long time. I was worried you might not find me... desirable," Gemma said, barely above a whisper. Not a young lady anymore, she was older, a little wiser, and she'd never been one of the prettiest girls in Midhurst, let alone London.

The fear that he'd replace her with someone new, a more beautiful woman was a fear she didn't want to admit, but it was there, clawing at her heart, making it hard to breathe. Would she be enough for a man like James? Or would he find her lacking? She'd never measured her worth in looks before, and certainly had never valued herself by a man's affections. That hadn't changed. But if James didn't want her, it would hurt. Deeply. The eleven years she'd spent in their secret courtship through letters would have been a waste, and the decent, eligible men she had turned down now were all married with wives and babes of their own.

Lightheaded with the sweet swell of heat in her body and the slow growing ache between her legs, she bit back a moan when James slid one hand down from her waist along her thigh. Struggling to catch her breath, she tried to paw his hand away in an effort to ease the effect it had on her senses. James slid his hand off her thigh, to cover her own protesting hand and guided it down to her own leg. With this simple switch of hands, she felt a little more in control. He led her hand downward onto the smooth tenderness of her inner thigh, stroking the silk against her skin. He made her caress herself, in the way she had only ever done when alone in her bath.

Her head spun and little tingles skittered beneath her skin just knowing that he wished to touch her there, to explore the hidden skin of her legs. She leaned back against his chest, and he stretched his fine long legs out on either side of her own. He surrounded her, enfolding her completely in his embrace. She resisted the urge to touch him back, even though she wanted to feel him and ensure he was real. Gemma put her other hand tentatively on his right thigh. The heavy muscles, strong beneath her grasp, sent slow ripples of heat through her and her heart jumped in her chest. The muscles beneath her hand tensed, and he shifted a little behind her.

"Not find you desirable? Gemma, you are breathtaking!" He pressed his lips on her throat in a kiss.

Then he laughed softly, and he moved his other hand up to caress her breasts. Her flesh tightened beneath his touch and Gemma drew in a deep breath. James pulled her back harder against him, and she felt something hard, his arousal against her backside. That, too, Mary had warned her about, how a man's groin area would stiffen when he was ready to take a woman to bed. The idea had been laughable at the time, but now Gemma's lungs burned and her hands shook at the thought. Would he want to take her to bed? Would he try tonight? Did she want him to?

Gemma was not a wanton woman, but she was tempted by this...rogue. The way he handled her, the way he knew just how to make her body flood with heat and desire.

Jasper's hand on her thigh started to coil her gown, raising it past her calves, up over her knee until bare skin was revealed. If he touched her any more this way, she would surely faint, fall right off the bench and ruin her best gown...but if he stopped, she was sure she would die from unfulfilled yearnings.

"James...I don't think we should..." she tried to

speak but he caught her chin with his hand and angled her head to the side so that he could kiss her on the lips.

It was Gemma's first real kiss. She remembered James kissing her once, long ago, when they'd been children. He'd caught her by the back door to the kitchens of Haverford and pressed his lips to hers. A brief flash of a smile later and he'd run off, leaving her to stand alone and confused by his actions. She hadn't much liked that kiss, but what respectable girl of ten years old would? Now though, everything had changed and James's kisses had too it seemed.

This was a true kiss, with melting fire and the sweet taste of passion's first bloom.

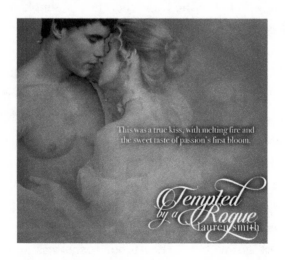

This was a true kiss, with melting fire and the sweet taste of passion's first bloom.

Tempted by a Rogue
Lauren Smith

His warm mouth on hers was a fascinating sensation. Soft lips that coaxed and teased, sending shivers through her in places she didn't know could tremble. When his tongue parted her lips and teased her own tongue, something deep in her belly twisted and clenched and a flash of heat shot through her like a fire in a pan. Quick, startling, making her gasp. She gripped his leg tighter, feeling the taut muscles of his thigh beneath her when she strained to kiss him harder. It would be so easy to lose herself in his arms, to the feeling of his mouth on hers. His lips twisted upward and he smiled between kisses.

"You taste divine, Gemma," he whispered huskily, as his hand drifted higher up her leg, straying close to dangerous areas.

She knew she should have tried to close her legs to prevent him from going further up. When his hand abandoned hers, it moved steadily onward beneath her gown, lifted her petticoats as though they weren't even there.

"Oh!" Gemma gasped when he stroked the tight coils of the dark triangle hidden between her legs. Tingles of pleasure shot up her spine, yet she squirmed a little at that touch, afraid of the mounting tension in her lower body. James caught her mouth with his, absorbing the little gasp, still smiling as he did so.

"I have waited years to touch you, Gemma..." he confessed in a soft sigh and nuzzled her cheek.

Gemma wanted to face him, wanted to see what she

knew had to be a handsome face. But he caught her hand as it strayed toward the blindfold, kissing the inside of her wrist, before moving her palm to his neck. She was able to twine her fingers in his silky hair and hold his head close to hers while he let his lips stray from hers down to her neck and then her shoulder. His hand between her legs moved a few inches deeper, caressing the entrance of her moist center and the violently pleasurable sensations that rippled through her made Gemma tremble. James paused in his deep caress to kiss her.

"Are you all right?" His touch gentled as he waited for her to answer.

Gemma tried to nod, but she still trembled. She knew if she tried to stand she'd sooner fall than walk. He pulled his hand away, seeming to realize just how affected she was.

"Gemma..." he cooed softly, his hand pulling her gown back down over her legs.

"James...I'm sorry. I'm not used to..." Gemma tried to explain herself, so ashamed that she wanted to sink into a hole in the ground and hide from him. She'd waited years for him, for this moment and now she was inexperienced and unsure of herself. Would he want a woman more experienced? Shame made her face heat and tingle. She closed her eyes, trying to breathe. Who would have thought her innocence would have become a burden?

"There's plenty of time for you to get used to this

and to me," his soft voice purred without the slightest hint of annoyance. He was compassionate to wait, to not press her until she had grown used to these new passions he'd lit within her body. How could she have ever thought to doubt his intentions?

When he got up and let go of her, the warm heat of his body vanished. The deprivation of his close proximity had a startling effect on her, she had to still her own arms from reaching out to bring him back into her embrace. Gemma turned around instinctively but the blindfold kept her ignorant of her love's appearance.

"Will you be at Lady Greenley's party tomorrow?" She tried to sound casual, as though he hadn't just changed her entire world in a matter of a few caresses and kisses.

"Yes, but promise me you will not speak a word of what has transpired tonight. Our meeting must be kept secret."

"A secret?" A flicker of insecurity flashed through her but she dispelled it. This was James! He would do right by her, there was no question of that.

"Yes, until I can ask you to marry me properly." James placed a tender kiss on her forehead and his footsteps retreated in the distance.

She pulled the blindfold off in time to see the tall fine figured back of a man with dark hair vanish around the garden's edge. Gemma clutched the beautiful blindfold to her chest, her entire body quivering with joy. James was going to marry her! To think that she would be blessed with years of tender words, and soft hot kisses...she was the luckiest woman in the world to know love at James Randolph's hands. The years of faithful affection they'd shared through words created by pens on paper had only made their future passion a mighty fire waiting for the chance to burn.

JASPER ARRIVED AT RANDOLPH HALL AND LEFT HIS horse with the groom. He was immediately granted entrance and shown into the evening room where James Randolph stood beside the marble fireplace, one hand braced on the mantle, swirling a glass of brandy. He didn't seem to be at all surprised at Jasper's arrival because he nodded toward a waiting glass of brandy on the mantle. It did nothing to ease the black mood that rolled through Jasper like summer storm clouds. Listening to Gemma gasp another man's name. James's name, made his blood burn. It should have been only Gemma and him in that garden without the specter of his friend between them.

"Jas, you devil, what took so long?" James asked, offering a second glass of brandy to him.

"I was delayed..." Jasper took the brandy from his friend and drank greedily.

"And your meeting with Gemma? How did it go? I'll wager that blindfold did the trick in disguising that it was you and not me who made love to her just now." James chuckled and sipped his brandy again.

It took everything for Jasper not to bloody his friend's nose. This whole scheme was dreadful and he despised the way it made his insides wither with guilt.

"James...are you sure you want to do this to her? I mean—"

His friend held up a hand to silence him. "Now, now, Jasper. Remember, we are in this tangle because *you* didn't do what I asked you to." James shook his head in reproach.

Unfortunately he was right, Jasper had done something incredibly foolish and now it was a thorn in his side to handle and a nasty blockade against James's marital plans. Not to mention Jasper's intentions to have Gemma for himself. Both he and James were trapped, one wanting to escape her and the other wanting to claim her with every fiber of his being. But there was no easy way of going about this. A man couldn't cry off an understanding even as fairly secretive as the one Gemma had, without a damned good reason. Ergo, she had to be compromised by another man, which would give James his honorable out, and hopefully Jasper would be able to swoop in and snatch her up.

I have to. She loves me, she just doesn't know it's me.

That was probably the worst part of this plan, convincing Gemma the man she loved wasn't James, so that she'd let him go on his merry way without her.

James had decided to get married after all, despite being the jaded lover he'd become to many a woman in many a port. He'd settled on some chit with a vile temper and an odious manner, but she turned a pretty ankle. That was all James cared about now, a lady's looks and her desire to have a bit of fun. Gemma was not the sort of girl James would have sought out for a bit of fun.

Gambling hells and boxing matches, and other lower forms of entertainment weren't something that would ever interest Gemma. She and James were so ill-suited it was a blessing the marriage between them would never happen, but it still wasn't fair that Gemma was being treated so poorly. Of course that was still Jasper's fault, he admitted that. It had been his letter writing that had left Gemma with hope of matrimony because he had every intention of marrying her, if she'd have him after what he'd done tonight.

"I wrote your letters to her like you asked me to, but I couldn't follow through with breaking her heart." Jasper flung himself into the nearest chair and glared up at James.

He knew they could have been mistaken for brothers, with their tall forms, dark hair and brown eyes. Each of them bore the fine proud features of the sons of English country gentry with sculpted chins, straight noses and strong jaw lines. The years spent toiling at sea had forged muscled gods of them and their newly won fortunes lent them both an air of recklessness that often resulted in trouble. More so for James than Jasper, of course.

"It's not my fault, Jas, that you couldn't let her down easy."

James was the more dramatic and outgoing of the two men, but he was not the leader between them. His flair for drama drew women to him, and he rather enjoyed the benefits of the opportunities this gave him. Jasper knew James had cared for Gemma Haverford when he was a boy, and he wrote to her sporadically that first year they were away at sea.

But by the time he'd reached seventeen, he'd fully immersed himself in womanizing like any decent rake, and no longer wanted to be burdened with the marital expectations of a dear, innocent little country girl like Gemma. James had therefore enlisted Jasper to pen a few letters to her pretending to be James and eventually break off the relationship.

However, Jasper had found he enjoyed his correspondence with Gemma, she had a ready mind and a quick wit and whatever worldly knowledge she lacked could easily be remedied. He never would have imagined she would become something he dreamt about every night, that her letters would get him through storms and fierce battles... Gemma, forever a sweet young girl in his eyes; an innocent country child who would never grow up...*had grown up*. And now the depth of his deception had him fairly torn in two where his loyalties were concerned. He would do whatever James

wanted without question, but Gemma? How strong was
that sweet child's hold on him, now that she was a sweet
woman? Too strong. So much so that he wanted to
marry her.

"So, did you see to it then?" James asked, smiling
crookedly at his friend.

"You mean, did I lure her into the garden and
compromise her?" Jasper's words came out more acidic
than they should have, but he couldn't help it, he was
not a fan of this whole wicked plot James had worked
up, which, given their rather reckless youth and daring
acts in the service of God, King and country, was saying
something.

"Well, did you?" James walked away from the fireplace and joined Jasper in the chair next to him.

"Take comfort in this, James. She is completely and
thoroughly compromised. The poor creature is so
madly in love with you that it will crush her tomorrow
when you call her out for being with another man."

Jasper's loyalties were uncomfortably tight at the
moment between his best friend of more than twenty
years and the girl to whom he'd been writing love letters
to for a decade. He wouldn't have agreed to James's
scheme if Gemma would have been truly hurt. The
worst of it would be a broken heart, and she'd recover
soon enough, and then he would win her for himself.
And James would be free to propose to Arabella
Stevens, his current "heart's delight," and intended
betrothed.

Jasper thought Arabella was nothing more than a fast little chit that James had met at Brighton. Unfortunately the girl had an uncle who lived only a few miles away from Midhurst. Jasper had no right to begrudge James his choice in women, he'd often sampled the pleasures of ladies of less than perfect reputation, but to marry one, when the likes of Gemma Haverford could be taken instead? It was nonsensical, completely, totally nonsensical. Of course now that he'd seen Gemma, well more than seen...he'd tasted her quite deeply...the thought of James standing at the altar with her made something in his gut churn uncomfortably. It was oddly reminiscent of when he'd been a lad out on the ship that first month, suffering from sea sickness.

"Excellent." James didn't seem even remotely concerned about Gemma and what Jasper might have done to her in the garden. In fact, it had been his idea for Jasper to do "more" than just meet with her.

"How was she? Our blushing country girl?" James smiled wickedly over the top of his brandy glass, brown eyes warm with mischief.

Jasper's brow furrowed as he debated on how to answer.

"She was very sweet, but she's completely green, poor thing. I barely touched her before she was shaking like a leaf. I didn't dare go all the way with her," Jasper said, a little wave of guilt rippled through him. He'd done a tad more than touch, but could anyone blame him? A ripe fruit hanging from a vine, he couldn't resist...

"A green girl? How is that possible at her age? No, wait, let me guess, she's too plump, and not at all attractive? Is she an ugly freckled little thing? She must be, with all that ginger hair I remember she had as a child." James chortled.

Jasper grimaced at his friend. He didn't like hearing Gemma talked about, especially in such a cruel manner. He didn't love her, that would be nonsense, but he did *care* about her, deeply, the way one does a favorite spaniel and he didn't like it when another man kicked his dog. He wanted to protect Gemma from the world, the way he would anything he cared about, even if it meant keeping James's callous remarks away from her little ears.

"You would be surprised, James. She's quite a beauty."

"Oh? Then why didn't you finish the deed, Jasper? We agreed..." James watched him curiously now.

Jasper clenched his fists automatically, his body aching to suddenly throw a vicious right hook into James's smug face. He forced his self-composure, uncoiling his tightened fists and relaxing again.

"She was so...I've never made a woman shake before James. I didn't like it, knowing that she was only letting me do those things to her because she thought I was *you*. She's kept herself for you, and I couldn't just rip that innocence from her in less than an hour." Jasper rubbed his eyes, wearily, as he tried to erase that creeping guilt again. Her voice, crying out James's name, echoed in his head and that nausea returned again. He wanted Gemma to love him, to know it was him and not James she'd kissed.

I must bide my time. Wait until all of this is done, then I shall go after her.

"How amusing...that she would affect you so. Perhaps you ought to have a go at her Jas, keep yourself entertained until I can secure Arabella," James mused and rubbed his chin.

"No, I've already damaged her enough. Almost making love to her while pretending to be you was bad enough. I won't do more than that."

"Aww, come on Jas, do a friend a favor. We both know what Gemma is like. She won't let our engagement drop without putting up a fight. I need you to entice her away and offer her something...sweeter." James looked at him pleadingly and Jasper huffed loudly.

"Sweeter? Good God, James, you want me to act the libertine to distract her away from you?" What a wretched notion, but he owed James.

"Jas, please. You know I can't marry Gemma. She's not what I want out of life. Not *anymore*." James met him with an even stare, and Jasper knew what his friend said was true. He didn't want love, didn't want that vulnerability it could give a man. They'd both seen men driven mad by love and James had made it clear years ago he wanted nothing to do with loving a sweet country girl like Gemma. Better to wed and bed a viper like Arabella and have no expectations of heartbreak. At least that was James's thinking, as far as Jasper knew and he knew his friend well.

Their friendship ran deep. James had risked his life more than once to save Jasper and he'd done the same in return. Over the boom of canons and through the fog of war, they'd stayed together, been wounded together. Their blood had run in twin rivers, mixing upon the floor of a cabin after a cannon ball had torn through the hull of their ship. That wasn't something easily dismissed when it came to a question of loyalty. But he did not want James to know how much he cared about Gemma. He didn't want his closest friend to make things difficult for him when he pursued Gemma.

"Fine, I'll keep her occupied so you can have your damned Arabella," Jasper said, watching his friend's pleading face turn to ecstatic excitement.

"Wonderful! I must write Arabella and tell her to be at the garden party tomorrow." James finished his brandy, and Jasper got to his feet.

"I'd best be going, before it gets too late," Jasper said and both men clasped hands. He left Randolph Hall, with the strange sensation he'd just made a pact with the devil to steal poor Gemma's innocence. He didn't like how that made his stomach churn. But promises were promises. With any luck, however, he would be able to make it up to Gemma by marrying her.

CHAPTER 3

It was nearly impossible to keep a secret. Especially one involving a relationship with a man. Gemma found that out in the most difficult way possible the morning following her meeting with James in the garden the night before. Only Mary, her lady's maid, had known she'd met with him in the maze-like sprawl of her father's country estate gardens. Still, it hadn't escaped her notice this morning that her mother hummed while they broke their fast and watched her with a devious twinkle in her eye.

"James arrived in town last evening, did you know that Gemma, dear?" her mother asked while she spread some orange marmalade over a slice of toast.

Good heavens, is nothing secret here? Gemma bit her lip before replying.

"He did? How wonderful! I take it he'll be sure to attend Lady Greenley's party today then."

The white painted door to their small breakfast room opened and Gemma's father, John Haverford strode in, a newspaper under one arm and a stack of letters in the other.

"Morning, my heart." He bustled over to her mother and kissed her cheek before he winked at Gemma. "Get a good night's sleep, Gemma?"

"Yes, papa, and you?"

"Oh yes. I almost went for a walk in the gardens, but thought better of it. The weather was nice though, wasn't it?"

She swallowed hard, choking on the bit of egg she'd just slipped in her mouth. Her father had almost come cross her and James in the gardens?

"Gemma, you're flushed, too much time in the sun this morning?" Her mother's concern was sweet, but Gemma knew she'd faint flat out if she guessed the real source of Gemma's high color.

"No, I just walked through the fields to the village and back, and not too fast." It was a lie, but not a bad one. She'd actually run through the fields for a bit before coming back home. She loved to run, there was something wicked and wild about dropping one's silly bonnet and just sprinting through the grass with only the wind as her companion. Last night had left her in such a wonderful mood that she hadn't been able to resist running most of the way back from Midhurst to her home this morning.

"I think it will be interesting to attend Lady Greenley's party today. I suspect there will be much to talk about Mr. Randolph and Mr. Holland's glorious return from the high seas." Her father laughed and settled down at the table across from her mother. He retrieved a pair of silver rimmed spectacles and perched them on the tip of his nose so he could read the paper he'd spread out beside his plate.

"Indeed," her mother agreed. "This town does know how to gossip, doesn't it?" Her mother chuckled.

The small market town of Midhurst barely held seven hundred people, and so naturally everyone knew *everything* about everyone else. From seventy-five year old Lady Edith Greenley, the highest level of Midhurst's society, right down to the poorest farmer's family, there were few, if any, secrets. Gemma knew this better than anyone, so she resolved to keep her mouth shut like James asked her to. She was excited to see him today at the Garden Party.

Every year Lady Greenley held a garden party, inviting all the local gentry and some of the better off merchant families to attend. Gossip was shared, tea drank, crumpets and scones devoured and engagements announced. There was an unmistakable stirring of pride in her breast that she would finally be able to count herself among the lucky women who had earned engagements. Of course, the secret of her soon-to-be-engaged state had left her rather more excited than was perhaps wise. She nearly bounced on her heels like an eager spaniel while she finished breakfast. After that, she dashed back upstairs where Mary helped her dress.

"Good luck, miss." Mary winked. "And don't be getting into too much trouble you hear? I'm afraid your hair won't stand for much mussing with this style."

"Thank you, Mary." Gemma giggled. James would have to behave whilst they were at the party, no sneaking off, however much she might want to do just that if he tried. It wouldn't do to come back to the party looking thoroughly compromised, even if the engagement was announced today.

"Will Mr. Randolph be speaking to your father?" Mary asked and handed Gemma a bonnet with lovely blue ribbons dangling down in silk tendrils.

"I..." She honestly didn't know. He'd have to, wouldn't he? But it would need to be done before the announcement so unless James met with her father at the party early, she might not have her engagement announced there. The thought was a depressing one.

Mary touched her arm gently. "There now, Miss, no need to worry. I'm sure your young man will have it all planned and proper."

"I hope so," Gemma whispered and then left her room to meet her mother at the entrance of the house to wait for their carriage to take them to Lady Greenley's. So much depended on how this party would go and she hated how excited she was to see James again. Eleven years was a long time to wait for a man to come home, a man she loved fiercely, with every part of her body and soul.

Her mother placed a calming hand on her arm to indicate she stop fidgeting. "Calm down dear, today will be a good day, I just know it."

Shooting a glance at her mother, she tried to smile. Her mother was the sort of woman who saw silver threading to every dark shadowed cloud, and could take any pie that was too tart, and find a way to sweeten its taste. Gemma had a tad more of her father's sardonic nature in her. In other words, she tended to fret, not too much of course, but enough every now and then that her mother would have to remind her not to be so restless with her worries.

"Mama, do you think James will..." She glanced down at herself, trying to see how she might look from his point of view.

Her mother's eyes twinkled. "He will." She didn't have to say anything more. Mothers had an uncanny way of doing that sometimes, seeing right through to their child's innermost thoughts.

"I hope so," she replied more to herself than to her mother and once more studied her appearance. She wore her best sprigged muslin gown and had her hair tamed into a respectable Hellenic fashion. But she had to heed Mary's warning and not let James muss her hair too much.

The carriage pulled up in front of the entrance and her father appeared just in time to assist her and Mama inside. As she settled into her seat, she clutched her reticle. Inside it she kept the blindfold cloth. It was a token of the passion she and James had shared. She felt a little foolish, but she'd never been so happy, so *in love* before. Without the presence of James there, Gemma pushed her mind to other thoughts, more specifically to thoughts of the letters James had written her.

For the first few years of his absence, his replies had been scattered and brief in subject matter, which she had attributed to his chaotic life at sea. But for the last several years his pace and length had changed. His penmanship had improved, as did his ability to express himself. She had begun to look forward to his monthly letters, hearing amusing anecdotes about his fellow sailors and harrowing adventures of foreign lands. His prose had often been poetic and deeply romantic toward the most recent few years of her letters. It had been such a dramatic change from the ill-expressed thoughts of a boy starting his life's journey to a man who'd lived a full exciting life and had learned much about himself and his fellow man. Life at sea had matured James greatly and she was never more ready to give herself to him in every way.

She hoped he would see marriage as the next great adventure. That love and someday children, could fill a void he'd not yet satisfied in his life. It was something she longed for, but only with him, not with any other man. No one else understood her the way he did, listened to her when she spoke of things, and when he agreed or disagreed, the discussion was always intelligent, frank and completely unguarded by fears of what the other would think. Of course, this had only been through letters, but she knew deep inside her bones that the man in the letters would be just as wonderful in reality. They had become partners in their thoughts, and now she wished more than anything to become partners fully in life.

The carriage took a narrow path through the wooded glen and past the village to the other side of Midhurst. Cutting through another small forest, the vehicle rumbled around a bend and a sweeping expanse of beauty stunned Gemma. No matter how many times she saw Lady Greenley's lands she was always amazed at the sheer effect it had on her.

The tan sandstone house sat atop a hill, the many windows reflecting the noon sunbeams, making the glass wink and sparkle like distant diamonds. A large lake lay below the house, the waters dancing with the light breeze, and golden rushes at the water's edge waved back and forth in slow ripples. A large lawn led to a garden maze much like her garden back home and colorful tents and tables already dotted the landscape of the lawn in the distance, appearing so small that they seemed more like colorful toadstools that fairies would sit upon during a midnight revelry.

When she and her parents arrived at Lady Greenley's grand estate entrance, her gaze swept expectantly over the milling crowds gathering on the vast lawn.

There was no sign of James, or even a tall dark-haired man who could be him. Perhaps he was deep in the garden, waiting for her to seek him out, or maybe he was running late, his horse having thrown a shoe.

A crowd of people exited the garden and gathered near the tables by the garden entrance. Two tall men stood with their backs facing her, talking with her fellow Midhurst neighbors. She knew the look of them right away, no other men of her acquaintance in this little town had such a striking appearance. James and Jasper were here. *Finally*. The boys of Midhurst had come home as men.

Against all her control, she smiled, fully, unable to contain it.

James. She sighed and grinned again like a silly girl still in the schoolroom.

"Gemma, your mother and I are off to the tea tables, we shall meet up with you later." Her father winked at her before he gently secured his wife's arm, tucking it into his while leading her to the nearest tent where a beleaguered young footman set out tea for the guests clustered around him.

Her father, no longer a young buck, still bore the vestiges of his youthful good looks, like her mother. As a pair, Gemma's parents looked lovely together. They inclined their heads toward each other and whispered softly. Her parents had been married for thirty-one years and were still loving and affectionate toward each other as ever. They had the sort of love and marriage born of years of friendship, passion, and now, deep love. She'd been blessed to have grown up in such a house, fostered with such love.

"Gemma dear!" a familiar feminine voice called out.

Lily Becknell, one of her dearest friends, strode toward her. Lily was the town's true beauty with fair blonde hair and blue eyes, with a soft womanly form that drew only admiration from every male eye when she passed. With Lily came a shorter woman with black hair and shiny little black eyes. It made Gemma think of a rat she'd seen in the gardens once, all beady black eyes and gnashing teeth. She shivered in revulsion at the memory. This stranger flashed Gemma a calculating sort of smile that caused an undercurrent of unease to move through her. It was not the type of look one young lady ought to give to another, not if they were meant to be on friendly terms.

"Lily! How are you?" She clasped hands with her friend and smiled politely at the other woman.

"Gemma, this is Miss Arabella Stevens. You recall a Mr. Stevens who lives a few miles north of Randolph Hall? This is his niece," Lily informed her.

"Oh yes, of course! Miss Stevens, it is so nice to meet you," Gemma greeted with genuine warmth. Mayhap the woman was nice once a person got better acquainted with her. Then again, perhaps not. Gemma bit her lip to hide her frown.

The other woman smiled, but it wasn't exactly a friendly expression when it was displayed on her face.

There was something almost vicious in the feral glint of the woman's dark eyes and her smile revealed teeth that smiled seemed gritted together as though in great displeasure. There was no way that Gemma would be able to keep from picturing that rat in the garden when she saw this woman.

"It is a pleasure to meet you, Miss Haverford," Arabella replied, her rosebud lips pinched into a little simper.

Rattish eyes and teeth aside, Gemma had to admit Arabella was attractive and dainty looking, nothing like Gemma with her fuller figure and taller body. Her father used to call her Little Diana because of her beauty and her strong looking form, like the Goddess of the Hunt. But men did not want such women, they wanted petite delicate flowers that depended upon them for protection. Men were silly though to toy with such flowers, for they often had the sharpest thorns. And Arabella looked very thorny indeed, at least to Gemma.

I should be ashamed to be so petty in my thoughts. She knew that, but she couldn't stop herself from thinking them. Sometimes a person simply didn't strike her as genuine and that always bothered Gemma.

Lily broke through Gemma's prickly thoughts. "Have you seen Mr. Randolph and Mr. Holland? They are just over there, talking to Lady Greenley." There was a hint of mischief in Lily's tone. She and only she, outside of Gemma, knew of the understanding between her and James.

"I have not..." She craned her head about toward the two tall men again, vastly distracted by their handsome forms. The way their navy overcoats and buckskin trousers molded to such strong, athletic forms. A little shiver rippled through her at the memory of touching James's muscles, particularly those of his thighs and the way it felt to clench them while she rode through a seemingly endless wave of pleasure at his knowledgeable hands.

"James came by my carriage, with my uncle of course," Arabella supplied to the conversation and Gemma's head snapped back to her. Why would this woman think she could take such a familiarity with James, when only Gemma had that right?

"Yes, it was kind of you to provide such transport for him," Lily added diplomatically. Gemma decided to believe what she wished, that Arabella had *no claim* to James. Perhaps Arabella's uncle lived near James's family home, and offered a ride out of kindness.

Yes, that was it. She couldn't help but smile. All would be well, she was going to see James. She turned back to her friend, seeking any bit of information about James, but she would have to ask about Jasper too, in order to prevent any speculation by Arabella that she and James had an understanding.

"Well Lily, how did you find them? Are they much improved from those darling boys of our youth who used to tug our braids and put frogs in our pinafore pockets?" Gemma ignored Arabella now, eager to hear what Lily had to say about the two prodigal men of Midhurst.

Lily smiled secretively and leaned in close and conspiratorially to Gemma. "Never have you seen such a finer pair of men. If I had not married my Henry last year, why I'd be setting my lures to catch one of them." Lily winked at her and Gemma suppressed a laugh. Lily had always gotten into arguments with the boys when they'd been younger, whilst Gemma had tried eagerly to catch up when the young men had run off on their much longer legs. The mere idea of Lily marrying either one of the two bucks was laughable. She'd spend too much time arguing with them if one of them ever became her husband.

"Oh really, Lily, you are too much!" Gemma smiled and bit her lip, looking over Lily's shoulder toward the pair of men again.

Turn around James, I want to see you, she silently begged. *Let me put a face to the dreams I've had for years. Let me see the lips that brought forth such passion last night.*

Lady Greenley's screech jerked Gemma out of her thoughts.

"You, Haverford! Come here at once!" Lady Edith Greenley's bonneted head bobbed up and down when she waved at Gemma and demanded she come to her like a general in His Majesty's army. The ancient yet formidable Lady Greenley stood near the two men, who both turned at Lady Greenley's shout, in order to see Gemma.

Her heart stopped and she sucked air into her burning lungs after what seemed like ages of being frozen in time. Funny, she'd never had this happen before in her life, but seeing the faces of James Randolph and Jasper Holland after eleven years... Her world spun on its axis, as though she were a celestial planet shifting in its orbit, thrown into a spin by seeing these men. Side by side, they stood, almost an equal height, proud and strong in looks and demeanor. And both of them stared directly at her, equally curious to see her as she was to see them.

The resemblance of the two men to each other was startling. Only her childhood memories dared to find differences between the manly faces turned toward her. James had a fuller mouth, quicker to smile, but Jasper, quiet, calm, Jasper had eyes like liquid caramel that smoldered so powerfully when he stared at her that her mind simply blanked of all thought.

A rapid play of inscrutable emotions danced across his eyes, touched lightly upon his mouth as though he nearly smiled, but caught himself. Why on earth would Jasper smile at her? When he'd been a boy he'd always avoided her and had shouted rudely at her more than once that she was a nuisance and ought to go home and practice her needlepoint and sketching rather than gallivant off into the wooded glens after him and James.

Not that I ever listened to him. She almost smiled back at Jasper. She had the strangest urge to needle him, challenge him for daring to smile at her.

LAUREN SMITH

"Now Haverford! I could keel over and die waiting for you to grace me with your presence," Lady Greenley snapped, prodding the ground with the tip of her closed parasol. Gemma excused herself from Lily and Arabella and walked quickly toward Lady Greenley. She tried not to stare at the men when she reached them.

"What can I do for you, Lady Greenley?" Gemma asked.

"Can I depend upon you to rescue me from these unruly young bucks? Take them about the garden, and see that they don't scandalize my party, won't you?" Lady Greenley demanded of Gemma, a wicked glint in the older lady's gray eyes. With her crafty mannerisms and being rather boisterous for her age, no one dared to cross her.

"Of course, Lady Greenley," Gemma answered politely.

Both men grinned at her. The direct attention from both James and Jasper heated her skin with an embarrassing blush. There was nothing decent in either of their gazes. She could understand a look like that from James, after what they had shared, but Jasper? He should not be eyeing her form with such a bold look of appreciation like he did at that exact moment.

Lady Greenley watched this odd triangle of looks with an arched brow of interest, and Gemma thought she saw the old woman hide the beginnings of a smile beneath her ridiculously foppish bonnet. Where James's gaze seemed to outline every curve of her body with speculation, Jasper's gaze had the deep sensual sweep of such force that she almost felt his *hands* stroking her rather than his eyes...it was a knowing gaze, like he knew just how the flesh of her breasts would tighten, her legs tremble and her breath quicken beneath his touch...

"Why, is that really you, Miss Haverford?" James exclaimed with a broad smile and a deep bow. It did little to dispel the ensnaring enchantment of Jasper's heated gaze which distracted her from James.

Gemma forced a soft laugh, letting James take her hand and kiss it, but the tingling rush of contact she expected did not come. His voice did not seem quite the same as the night before, perhaps because it was disguised by his whispering tone...

"Mr. Randolph, Mr. Holland, I'm so glad to see you both returned to Midhurst in good health." Her gaze was strangely drawn back to Jasper, who watched her in deep concentration and she didn't know what to make of his scrutiny. She nibbled her bottom lip, studying Jasper intensely. His shoulders were wide...a little wider than James's now that she compared them so diligently.

James dropped her hand and glanced between her and Jasper, one brow raised.

"Er...we're quite glad to be home, Miss Haverford," James added, trying to draw her attention again. "I see Midhurst has treated you well over the years, Gemma." His voice deepened, but still Gemma didn't tear her gaze away from Jasper.

Was it possible to have a battle between a man and woman based on eye contact alone? She did feel as though she were battling this man, what she couldn't understand was why. His lips twitched, her eyes narrowed and her heart gave a strange little flip in her chest when his gaze lowered, inch by inch to focus on her lips.

We're strangers, after all these years. I should not be fascinated by him.

When he spoke to her, however, her body responded with a terrifying thrill of recognition.

"You are looking well, *Gemma*." The way he caressed her name...she went suddenly pale. That voice! Jasper's voice was the voice in the garden, the voice that belonged to the body which had...

No, no! He could not be the man I... Gemma wavered on her feet when a cloud seemed to cover her mind and she couldn't quite control her legs enough to stay standing.

"Now you've done it you rogues! Gone and frightened the girl. Shame!" Lady Greenley struck Jasper in the chest with the pointed end of her parasol.

Jasper grunted with the impact of the parasol's blow to his navy waistcoat and doubled over as though in pain. James ducked when Lady Greenley's parasol whirled through the air where his head had been moments before.

"Have at you, you devils!" Lady Greenley cried, waving the parasol aloft like a saber as she started forward to continue the attack.

Both men got control of themselves and flashed smiles in Gemma's direction and looks of amused fright at the crazy, old battle-axe before turning tail and running toward the garden like any sensible rogues would do when threatened by the likes of such a woman aiming a parasol at their jugulars. Once Lady Greenley had clearly vanquished them, at least enough that they had sought safe haven in her garden, Lady Greenley turned to face the recovering Gemma.

"Now, Haverford, what's all this fainting nonsense? Tell me what's gotten your shift in a twist?" the elderly lady demanded in an all-knowing whisper. Had Gemma not grown up around Lady Greenley, the bold vulgarity of her reference to undergarments would have been shocking and not amusing. But this was Lady Greenley after all and no one would be surprised at her wild behavior after knowing her a short time.

Lady Greenley was far too smart for her age and saw far too much. Gemma shook her head, not wanting to breathe a word of what she'd discovered, especially if those words spread, as they often did in Midhurst. She still couldn't believe it. Jasper, not James, had met her in the garden, had deceived her, had compromised her... Why? How? A thousand questions beat inside her mind so harshly that it made her eyes ache and she shut them, rubbing them with gloved fingertips for a few moments while she struggled to regain her composure.

If James knew the truth, knew that she'd been compromised by another man, his best friend no less...

knew that it was Jasper who had kissed her, touched her... It didn't matter that she thought it was James the whole time, he would not forgive her.

Fury boiled inside her. She distinctly remembered saying 'James' in the garden, several times, and her 'love' had not corrected her. He had wanted her to believe he was James! Lady Greenley was right. Jasper, at least, was a rogue. Not a good one either, not the sort of rogue a woman would sigh and swoon over then whisper about in giggles to her friends. But not Jasper. He was the sort of rogue who would end up on a dueling field, likely shot for having stolen his best friend's future wife's virtue. A wave of nausea followed her churning fury.

"Excuse me Lady Greenley, I have a man to strangle," she growled softly and started off toward the garden where she'd seen both men flee. She was going to find Jasper and ring his bloody neck. After that, she was going to cry for a very, very long time.

"Remember dear, use both hands, cuts off their air quicker!" Lady Greenley's advice warbled across the lawn when she cut through the garden's entrance. At any other time in her life, Gemma would have been fascinated to stay and hear just how Lady Greenley had gained such useful knowledge of the strangulation of rogues, but not today.

DYING TO KNOW WHAT HAPPENS NEXT? GRAB THE book HERE!

OTHER TITLES BY LAUREN SMITH

Historical

The League of Rogues Series

Wicked Designs

His Wicked Seduction

Her Wicked Proposal

Wicked Rivals

Her Wicked Longing

His Wicked Embrace

The Earl of Pembroke

His Wicked Secret

The Last Wicked Rogue

Never Kiss A Scot

The Earl of Kent

Never Tempt a Scot (coming 2020)

The Seduction Series

The Duelist's Seduction

The Rakehell's Seduction

The Rogue's Seduction
The Gentleman's Seduction
Standalone Stories
Tempted by A Rogue
Bewitching the Earl
Seducing an Heiress on a Train
Devil at the Gates
Sins and Scandals
An Earl By Any Other Name
A Gentleman Never Surrenders
A Scottish Lord for Christmas

Contemporary
The Surrender Series
The Gilded Cuff
The Gilded Cage
The Gilded Chain
The Darkest Hour
Love in London
Forbidden
Seduction
Climax
Forever Be Mine

Paranormal
Dark Seductions Series
The Shadows of Stormclyffe Hall
The Love Bites Series
The Bite of Winter

His Little Vixen (coming early 2020)

Brotherhood of the Blood Moon Series

Blood Moon on the Rise (coming soon)

Brothers of Ash and Fire

Grigori: A Royal Dragon Romance

Mikhail: A Royal Dragon Romance

Rurik: A Royal Dragon Romance

Sci-Fi Romance

Cyborg Genesis Series

Across the Stars

The Krinar Chronicles

The Krinar Eclipse

The Krinar Code by Emma Castle

Buy these books today by visiting www.
laurensmithbooks.com
Or by visiting your favorite ebook/paperback book
store!

ABOUT THE AUTHOR

Lauren Smith is an Oklahoma attorney by day, author by night who pens adventurous and edgy romance stories by the light of her smart phone flashlight app. She knew she was destined to be a romance writer when she attempted to re-write the entire *Titanic* movie just to save Jack from drowning. Connecting with readers by writing emotionally moving, realistic and sexy romances no matter what time period is her passion. She's won multiple awards in several romance subgenres including: New England Reader's Choice Awards, Greater Detroit BookSeller's

**Best Awards, and a Semi-Finalist award for the
Mary Wollstonecraft Shelley Award.**

To Connect with Lauren, visit her at:
www.laurensmithbooks.com
lauren@laurensmithbooks.com
Facebook Fan Group - Lauren Smith's League
Lauren Smith's Newsletter

Never miss a new release! Follow me in one or more of
the ways below!

facebook.com/LaurenDianaSmith

twitter.com/LSmithAuthor

instagram.com/Laurensmithbooks

bookbub.com/authors/lauren-smith

CPSIA information can be obtained
at www.ICGtesting.com
Printed in the USA
BVHW081540231221
624752BV00009B/471

9 781947 206861